Beauty Sleep

OrangeBooks Publication

Smriti Nagar, Bhilai, Chhattisgarh - 490020

Website: **www.orangebooks.in**

First Edition, 2022

ISBN: 978-93-92878-56-5

Beauty Sleep

Dr. Lakshmi Muthukumar

OrangeBooks Publication
www.orangebooks.in

Dedication

I would like to dedicate my first novel, *Beauty Sleep*, to my dear father, Late Shri A.R. Subramanian, who instilled the love for reading in me. It saddens me, Appa, that I cannot place the first copy of the book in your hand.

To my dear father-in-law, Late Shri N. Subramanian, who was more a father figure than a father-in-law and my dear mother-in-law, Late Smt. Laxmi Subramanian, whose quiet presence and support was always an inspiration. Both of you, Appa and Amma, are sorely missed.

To my dearest mother, Smt. Rajalakshmi Subramanian, who has taught me all I need to know about life and has imparted in me the values of discipline, hard work and commitment. I am what you have made me Amma. Love you lots. Thanks for always being there.

To my loving husband, Kumar, whose unstinting support and feedback has always encouraged me to follow my dreams.

To my ever-supportive, dearest daughters, Disha (for her careful and painstaking proof reading) and Divya (for the beautiful cover page that adorns the novel). Thank you my sweethearts for all your love and motivation.

Acknowledgements

This book has been long in the making, inspired by a genre that has always fascinated me – the murder mystery. I would like to thank my editor, Sucharita Datta Asane for taking time to give her feedback painstakingly. Thanks are due to my aunt, Smt. Jayalakshmi Narayanswamy, for her meticulous comments on the timeline and also to a retired colleague from the Department of Chemistry, Dr. Balakrishnan for his assistance with some technicalities. And finally, I owe thanks to my dear family, my mother, Smt. Rajalakshmi Subramanian, my husband, Kumar and my daughters, Disha and Divya, for their love, support and patience.

Saturday, 24th April

10:45 a.m.

Rosy Fernandes walked in fifteen minutes late for an appointment that she had taken a week ago for 10:30 a.m. "Good morning, ma'am," Renu, the hair stylist greeted her warmly.

"I have an appointment for a facial, a head massage and a hair wash too." she said.

"It might be better to go in for the head massage first, then the facial and finally go in for the hair wash, what do you suggest ma'am?" Renu politely suggested.

"Hmm…that's fine," said her client and started leafing through the pages of one of the magazines kept on the stand beside the sanitizer. Renu was a good judge of what kind of a mood her customer was in. If she did not proactively indulge in small talk with the salon staff, it was a signal that they should keep mum and just do their job. In these pandemic times, it was a blessing there were clients still visiting their parlour after the lockdown. She adjusted her mask and quietly sanitized her hands.

"Are you going to do the facial for me today?"

"No, madam, Akshara will be doing the facial for you. She will do just as good a job. Don't worry," Renu reassured her as she poured some warm oil into a tiny bowl for the head massage.

“Thanks. Shall I change?”

“In here, ma’am. Let me help you.”

By the time Rosy had hung up her white T-shirt, skirt, bra and scarf neatly behind the door, Renu was ready and waiting to administer the head massage.

The herbal smell of the aromatic oil made Rosy Fernandes grimace, but the results were always great and the head massage restful and soothing.

She glanced at the lady on the adjacent chair, who was leafing through a women’s magazine as she waited for her colour to set, and realized that it was the rather pungent odour of the hair colour, more than that of the herbal oil, that was making her squirm.

Trying her best to relax, Rosy had just settled into a daydream, when Renu’s polite voice broke into her slumber, “Madam, I am going to start the steam now.”

The steam on her scalp made her perspire. She asked for some tissues to wipe out the sweat that was streaming down her forehead in large droplets. In about ten minutes the timer on the steamer pinged – time for the facial that Rosy had been waiting for.

“Your head massage is done. I hope you liked it ma’am?” Renu enquired politely.

Rosy nodded. “Please get me some water and tea to drink before I go for the facial. I would like to use the restroom as well.”

Renu bustled out of the cabin to prepare the cup of tea.

When she returned, she found that her client was still inside the toilet. She placed the tray containing the water and tea noisily on the side-table inside the cabin and trudged back.

Akshara, who had been assigned the facial at the last minute, was ready and waiting impatiently for her client. Finally, at around 12:15, Rosy Fernandes emerged from the restroom, drank water, had tea and then lay down on the bed ready for her facial. With an audible sigh, Akshara glanced at the clock as she began applying the aromatic cleansing lotion in firm circular motions on Rosy Fernandes' face. It was 12:20 p.m.

With the soft instrumental music playing in the background and the extremely relaxing facial that would last for at least an hour, Rosy Amelia Fernandes felt as if she was in seventh heaven. This was life! Time almost stood still. Suddenly, Rosy grimaced because of the extra pressure along her neck and shoulder muscles. "Ouch!" She hissed, "Gently!"

"Yes, madam. I'm so sorry. I will be careful."

Rosy Fernandes relaxed again. Once the facial began there was nothing to do except revel in that blissful state and sleep.

As Akshara applied the cleansing lotion to her client's face, her hands moving in synchronized motions and her thoughts anxiously turned towards her mother who had recently been diagnosed with a tumour in her uterus. Her brother had just called asking her to take leave and help him out as he could not handle it alone. Her sister-in-law did not share the best of relationships with her mother-in-law and Akshara knew that there would be tension brewing on the home front for her elder brother. She knew this was not the right time to ask Clara madam for any leave as the spa was already short staffed, but she would have to do it. She decided to broach the topic after working hours, at the end of the day.

After applying the cleanser, she switched on the steaming machine. It had a nozzle attached to it that allowed one to direct steam in the direction of the T-zone which was where most blackheads and whiteheads were lodged. Within a couple of minutes of steam, Akshara noticed that her client was coughing and sputtering, almost as if she was going to throw up. Her eyes started to water and her face turned a bright red. Her nose started watering. She looked as though she were gagging.

"What happened, madam? Are you unwell? Shall I get you a glass of water?"

Her client was rummaging desperately in her handbag for something. Finally, she seemed to find what she was looking for – an inhaler, one that Akshara had seen many asthmatic patients use.

In a state of panic, the client thrust some capsule into the inhaler, inhaled from it, struggling to breathe all the while. Nothing seemed to work. She was choking. Alarmed, Akshara turned the steamer off and bolted out of the cabin to fetch Renu. This was a nightmare!

By the time Akshara and Renu hurtled into the cabin, Rosy Fernandes was already on the floor, motionless, surrounded by some currency notes that had spilled out of her handbag, its contents all over the place.

"Oh my God! What on earth has happened here? Clara madam, please call a doctor!" Renu resisted the urge to scream. She kept her nerve and decided it was wise to keep her voice as low as possible and avoid drawing the attention of the sole customer in the spa other than Rosy Fernandes.

Clara D'Souza, the salon's proprietor, was aghast. What had happened in the cabin? She would have to keep her wits together, not lose control or her calm. "Send for Dr. Mhaske. Call his residence. He would not have reached the clinic yet. He lives in the building nearby. Actually, wait. I will call him."

Clara's hand trembled slightly as she searched for Dr. Mhaske's number on her cell phone. He responded after a few rings. "Doctor Mhaske? This is Clara D'Souza. From the spa. There is an emergency with one of my clients. She seems to be having trouble breathing and has become unconscious. Can you please come immediately?" She listened intently then muttered, "Thank you, doctor."

Although Clara had sent for the doctor, the sight of Rosy Fernandes did not give her much hope. She did not look like she was having difficulty breathing. In fact, she did not look like she was breathing at all. Gingerly, she walked around the prone figure then turned towards Akshara, who was trembling like a leaf.

“Now, while we are waiting for the doctor to arrive, Akshara, don’t panic and tell me exactly what happened.” Her voice was firm and patient. She was a strong woman and had faced many ups and downs in her life, but this was a first.

“Everything was fine, madam. I gave her steam after applying the cleanser. As soon as the steam got to her face, Ms. Fernandes started coughing then started searching for something desperately in her handbag. I will show you what it was,” said Akshara, even as she reached for the inhaler lying near the bag.

“No!” said Clara. “Don’t touch anything. Was the steamer cleaned this morning?”

Akshara replied, “No ma’am. It was cleaned yesterday just before the last client had her facial. In fact, that client insisted on it being cleaned thoroughly because she was allergic to dust.”

Using a glove, Clara opened the steamer’s valve. There was some water left over after the steam had been administered. There were dust-like particles floating in it. She did not want the hygiene in her parlour being questioned. That would mean additional trouble. She cleaned it thoroughly and replaced it with fresh water. Her mind was working overtime. “Akshara, don’t mention this to anyone. I do not want anyone to say that our spa is unhygienic. People can blame us for anything. I have to protect my staff as much as I need to protect the reputation of the salon.”

Dr. Mhaske was middle-aged, had a bushy moustache and a deep baritone. As soon as he walked into the parlour, Clara led him to the sole cabin in the spa which she reserved for facials and massages. The other staff members waited in the foyer. The sight that greeted Dr. Mhaske was not a pleasant one. He surveyed the scene – the currency notes, the purse and its contents scattered all over the floor – and reached for the lady's pulse. Grimly, he placed the stethoscope to her chest, listened for a while and turned towards Clara. "I am afraid your client is dead, Mrs. D'Souza. You will have to inform the police."

Clara and her staff were astounded. This was unexpected. What was the police going to think when they came in? "Lord in high heaven!" thought Clara to herself. "What on earth is happening?" She hastily collected herself and said, "Yes, doctor, of course." She led the doctor out of the cabin and shut the door. Politely, she requested him to have a seat and asked Renu to make him a cup of tea. Her mind was racing. She would have to send her other client home before the police arrived. No client of hers should interact with the police. It would be very bad for her business. Her spa was not very spacious. Though small, it was very dear to her. The pandemic had already been a huge setback. She did not want to get embroiled in a police case. She surveyed the tiny foyer with three chairs on its right and one on the left completely equipped with a mirror in front. On the extreme right was a wash basin. Behind the foyer was a small passage that led to three separate cabins. There was just one toilet on the extreme left. That was all the space there was. If the police walked in on a client, it would be embarrassing. Come what may, she had to avoid such an eventuality.

She then dialled 100 and briefly stated the facts. Clara had a sinking feeling that seemed to paralyze her. A client dead in her salon! She was not prepared for this. She tried her best to gather her wits together, trying not to think of the consequences of this unfortunate occurrence on her business. While they waited for the police to respond, Dr. Mhaske was getting impatient, but as the physician who had announced the person dead, he could not just leave without speaking to the police. In the meanwhile, he watched Clara D'Souza address her staff calmly:

"We must not show any alarm or panic in our voices when we speak to the police. There is no need to volunteer unnecessary information or generate any gossip. Also, Renu, cancel the rest of the appointments for the day. Say that due to some sudden carpentry work that has come up, madam has decided to close the salon for a few days. Ask them to reschedule their appointments. We can make home visits instead."

Renu walked in anxiously in a couple of minutes, "Madam, if I wash Mrs. Datta's hair colour off now the entire exercise will be a waste. The colour needs at least three hours to set."

Clara sighed impatiently, "Explain the situation to her, Renu. Tell her that there has been a medical emergency. It is better she washes the hair colour off her hair after going home. Tell her we need to shut shop early today. Be polite. I don't want to lose my existing clients."

Clara now turned to the other pressing problem at hand. She had tampered with the water in the steamer but that was only to ensure that they were not caught in any unnecessary controversy. They had not done anything wrong. They had nothing to fear, but as she explained the situation to her staff and how they should behave during the police interrogation, she could see the grim look on their faces. By this time, the sole customer in the spa had been cajoled into going home.

Akshara was already feeling faint. She knew that she would be questioned repeatedly. She was the one who had administered the facial, so the police would pay particular attention to her. She felt like throwing up.

By the time Clara had briefed her staff and Renu had explained the situation to their clients over the phone, a pall of gloom had descended on the parlour. Clara ensured that no one entered the cabin. With currency notes lying scattered all over the cabin floor, she could not take any chances.

When the police arrived, they were greeted by a solemn group of girls, a stoic Clara and an impatient, visibly irritated Dr. Mhaske.

1:32 p.m.

The police jeep pulled over in front of the footpath just outside *Casablanca Arcade*, the complex that housed *Clara's Spa*. The spa had a stylish signboard and a neat, well-maintained porch. As Inspector Pramod Talpade, Havaldar Shetty and the forensic expert-cum-cameraman, Ashutosh Dubey, entered the beauty parlour, the uniformed staff formed a protective ring around Clara.

"Sorry for the intrusion, ladies. No one will leave the premises till we have interrogated each and every one of you. So, please cooperate," announced the Inspector. As he entered the spa, his attention was caught by the eye of the metallic fish holding a coin in its mouth, staring defiantly at him. It reminded him of the *Matsya* avatar from the *Dashavatar* as depicted in the *Amar Chitra Katha* comics he had read in his childhood.

"Please ask all your customers and staff to wait patiently till our interrogation is over, Mrs. D'Souza. Now take me to the dead body."

"There are no clients present here inspector. Only our staff is here. Rosy Fernandes was the first client for the day. We cancelled the other appointments for the day and sent the clients who were already here home after what happened in the morning." Even as she uttered these words, Clara ushered the inspector and his team into the cabin. Inspector Talpade looked visibly perturbed, "*Kaay boltaay* madam? You cannot just send your customers home. Call them immediately and ask them to come for questioning. Everyone who was here needs to be interrogated."

Clara nodded. She knew she would have to obey orders.

The inspector carefully surveyed the cabin. Rosy Fernandes lay balled up on the floor, as if she had been fumbling with something in her handbag at the moment when death struck her unexpectedly. The handle of her handbag was still loosely clutched in her finger, as if she had made a last-minute attempt to retrieve something from it. The contents of the handbag had, however, fallen all over the floor and the scene was made unforgettable by the number of currency notes that lay scattered all around the cabin. Talpade whistled softly. There must be at least fifty thousand in cash here.

The dead woman was wearing a black robe. Her hair was short and wavy. Her mouth was open and some saliva had drooled from its corner. Her eyes were open in what seemed to be a fixed stare at the wall. Talpade signalled to Ashutosh Dubey, who proceeded to collect a sample of the saliva for analysis.

Most of the saliva had already started to dry up, but there was still some drool in the open mouth of the victim moist enough to be tested. After collecting the sample, Dubey started clicking the official pictures.

A quick survey of the stuffy cabin revealed a steamer with a 15-inch long white plastic nozzle, which could be pointed in any direction, attached to what seemed like a steaming machine. There was a small wash basin on the left-hand corner with a huge mirror. A trolley with drawers was placed beside the wash basin and contained items such as combs, sponges, hair brushes and various pastes and powders. He moved swiftly towards the door of the cabin and shut it to see what the cabin looked like from the inside when the door wasn't open. Three hooks held plastic hangers which had hanging on them a scarf, a bra, a black skirt and a smart, white ladies top. His preliminary enquiries revealed that the clothes belonged to the dead client. A woman of neat habits, he thought to himself, judging from the carefully folded manner of the clothes. Most people would have hung their clothes any which way.

An overpowering odour of some fruity cosmetic hung over the cabin and the unmistakable aroma of a room freshener, typically out of an aerosol, probably lavender, the inspector thought. He looked at the victim's toes and fingers for signs of a struggle. He had to ensure that any possible DNA that could be collected from under the fingernails of the victim was sent to the Forensics Department for analysis. Usually, the skin or hair of the attacker could be found under the victim's nails in case of a struggle. However, there seemed to be none in this case. The fingernails on her feet and hands were carefully manicured and painted. She was in her early thirties and seemed to have preserved herself very well.

Her fingers still clutched what seemed like an expensive, branded handbag. One of the compartments in its centre was open and a slim, blue, steel flask peeped out of it. Inspector Talpade pulled his gloves on tighter as he unzipped the other two compartments of the bag.

He rummaged through the contents of the bag, but they were typical of any woman's bag - a lipstick, a nail file, a hairbrush, a compact, a couple of debit cards and visiting cards in a wallet, a cheque book, a pass book, a tiny pouch that contained some jewellery (a ring and a chain, probably ones that she had removed at the salon), a set of keys, a mobile phone, some medicines, an inhaler, a small bottle containing some capsules and a charger.

He jotted down her residential address from the *Adhaar* card and made a mental note of it as his next stop after he had checked the crime scene. He would have to process the necessary papers and get a warrant to examine her residence. As he rifled through the visiting cards, one card caught his attention. It was Rosy Fernandes' own visiting card – *Rosy Fernandes, Secretary to the CEO, Advent Electronics.* This was a lead he would have to pursue.

"Has any doctor examined the lady?" asked the inspector.

"Yes sir," replied Clara. "Our local GP, Dr. Mhaske is here and he has already taken a look at her. He was the one who pronounced her dead."

Dr. Mhaske had been waiting impatiently all this while. Now he suddenly sprang into attention, secretly thrilled with all the excitement. He was, albeit momentarily, taking centre stage and enjoying his moment in the sun. "Dr. Shrikant Mhaske. I live in the adjacent colony. The parlour staff usually comes to me for their routine medical complaints." The doctor held out his hand.

"I see. What do you think, doctor? What seems to be the cause of death?" Inspector Talpade enquired even as he shook the proffered hand.

"Well, inspector, there is no bluish mark around or on her lips and primarily her facial expression is contorted and suggests some kind of difficulty in the respiratory tract that she must have experienced. Perhaps she has a history of asthma. I did ask the girl who was doing the facial for the lady and she mentioned that the client was uncomfortable with the steamer being on. You might get a better idea of her medical history if you can figure out who her family doctor was." Dr. Mhaske packed his bag and addressed the inspector, "I think my work here is done. You will be sending the body for a post mortem anyway and I think it will corroborate my preliminary findings. If there is nothing else, I will take your leave now."

"Please state your findings on your letter head, doctor. Do you have one with you now? Also, please ensure that you don't leave the city for a few days. We might need to interrogate you if we want to discuss the case or our findings."

Anxious to get out of the place, Dr. Mhaske nodded, quickly scribbled down his findings, handed over the paper to the inspector and left quietly. He was better off without such exciting incidents in his life.

Now that the doctor had left, inspector Talpade turned his attention once again to the cabin's entrance. It was quite cramped. The metal trolley bed had four drawers. Between the door and the bed there was just enough space for one person to comfortably enter. But first things first. He had to finish the interrogation.

He turned to the salon owner, Clara D'Souza. By the time he had finished interrogating her, Havaldar Shetty had already lined up the staff. Talpade could hear his booming voice in the background insisting that they wait patiently and cooperate. It was almost 3 pm and he still had to question the staff.

"Okay, now listen carefully everybody. I am inspector Talpade from the Bandra West Police Headquarters. Answer all the questions I ask you as truthfully as possible. Any attempt to withhold any information will land you in trouble with the law, so please co-operate. Is that clear?"

Clara D'Souza quietly stepped forward and on behalf of her staff, she said, "Sir, I assure you, they will cooperate to the best of their ability."

The officer announced loudly so everyone on the premises would hear him, "Do not leave town for any reason till this investigation has ended, understood, all of you?"

The body was sent for post mortem and Talpade started collecting everyone's fingerprints and documents to establish their identities, even as the interrogation progressed. Ashutosh Dubey, Talpade's assistant, had already dusted the cabin for fingerprints and had cordoned off the cabin with police tape. He was busy clicking pictures for their records.

Talpade turned to the spa's owner, who looked pretty agitated with all the mess around her. "The salon will not function till we are done, Mrs. D'Souza. We might need to revisit the scene so it will be sealed and closed. It could be homicide. We cannot say anything for sure till the post mortem report arrives. Do you understand? Also please inform the other customers who were present during the incident to report to the police station tomorrow so that we can record their statements."

Clara D'Souza nodded. Her business was going to be badly hit by all this. This was so unfair. Just when things had begun to go well.

Thursday, 8th April

6 a.m.

Once more, she had lied to her best friend. Another email dashed off, carefully composed, with no tell-tale traces that would betray the hollow life she actually led. That she was hiding something from Akhila was unimaginable for Prerna. Nostalgia flooded the moment. Tears welled up making it impossible for Prerna to see another word. The mail was auto-saved in drafts and she forced herself to take her routine walk around the garden in their housing complex.

As if the habitual exercise would give her an escape route.

All she did was walk around in circles. Wasn't all of life a futile uphill exercise? Why had she even considered the possibility that she should run away from herself? Change her fate? What was she thinking? The indelible imprints left behind on her psyche by the orphanage were never going to desert her. It was always Akhila who gave her the brief respites from bitter reality. Akhila, her best friend at the orphanage. Both of them suffered the same fate. But Akhila never settled for less. She always refused to accept the broken, bitten cookie. Akhila, the Fun. She created spaces where only walled prisons seemed to exist. She was no horseman or military leader like the legendary king of the Hunnic

Empire after whom she was named, but she did possess a commanding presence or so it seemed to the girls at the hostel housed within the Lok School Campus. Located within 100 yards of the school, the hostel was run by Mr. Parag Shah, a middle-aged man to whom the Patel family had entrusted the responsibility of managing the school's outreach programme, a community service – *Nirman*, a home for Destitute Women and their children.

The Patels were old money. Generations and legacies later, they still had enough to feed and clothe orphans whom the State did not care to acknowledge. Mr. Parag Shah was the only face of the Patel family the girls at the orphanage saw and heard. The Patels rarely visited. It was Mr. Shah who trained the girls to say, in unison, after every meagre meal of overcooked rice with a runny dal ladled carelessly over it, "Wow! What a delicious meal!" He would record mealtimes and change the lines that they had to utter. It was Mr. Shah who made them plant a kiss on his face before they left for school saying, "Good children must study hard and practice good habits." Although the four year olds knew no better, they hated the smell of pan that emanated from the man even when he stood a foot away. They would not get to wear the school uniforms that were ironed, folded and neatly stacked in a cupboard at the end of their dormitory. Those were reserved for special occasions, when the Patels came to visit or when the press came to photograph the place. It was Mr. Shah who kissed them goodnight as he tucked them in every night. He was the "father figure" who fondled them in bed and told them stories as he did so. They knew no better.

The only window in Prerna's room overlooked the garden in her housing society. A sprawling garden, it was diligently maintained by a gardener for whom tending plants was a passion that went beyond being a means to an end. What else could have motivated the man to report unfailingly before daybreak and water every shrub, bush and sapling? She marvelled at his zeal and dedication every day as she nursed her cup of tea brewed with ginger and lemon grass. This was a time of the day she cherished. The air was crisp and fresh, punctuated with just the sounds of birds chirping and sounds of water sloshing against four wheelers as the car-wash boys gave the vehicles parked all around the garden forming a metal corridor of sorts; a stark contrast to the green in the centre. Prerna tore herself away from the memories that haunted her and set out on her morning walk.

The artificial, sculpted mushrooms loomed majestically, covering the seating surface on either side; the hillock in the centre rose like a highpoint offering the best view and ventilation. In the evenings, it was the most coveted spot with senior citizens vying with the young adults to make it their rendezvous zone. At 6:30 in the morning, the hillock wore a deserted look with only the colony's strays curled up, dozing blissfully, on the two half-mooned wooden seats. Every parked two and four wheeler sported a garland of marigolds that hung limply, on the verge of wilting, the brilliant yellow and orange flecked with brushstrokes of a dull black that foreshadowed the end of their existence. As she turned the bend, her eyes were drawn towards a shrub that sported an entire bunch of marigolds as if they had suddenly bloomed on just that one patch. She paused, amazed at the sight. Then, wistfully, she saw it for what it really was. One of the car-wash boys had ingeniously draped a *toran* on top of the shrub to make it appear as if they were marigolds in full bloom. They resonated with her as a metaphor for her own life. As the watchman greeted her, she was jogged out of her reverie and resolve. Mounting the stairs towards the lift, she adjusted her glasses, as the sweat trickled behind her ears, and pressed 7.

Prerna involuntarily fluffed up the cushions on the sofa and shifted her attention to the centre table. It had invoices and printouts that her husband, Hemant, had left in disarray, with a box file functioning as a makeshift paper weight. With a sigh she stacked the papers in a neat pile and filed every one of them. The ashtray was filled with cigarette stubs, proof of a late night prep before an auditor's visit. Now that the centre table looked respectable enough, she moved towards the mantelpiece. As she dusted the curios that had been collected over the last twenty years as memoirs of trips overseas, her gaze fell on the framed picture which seemed to mock her. It was a nice picture. Anyone who saw it would assume that it was a handsome couple, made for each other. Hemant looked smart with a shock of hair that was reminiscent of a yesteryear Bollywood hero. She was no less. With an enviable mane of hair arranged in an elegant French bun, she looked resplendent in a bottle green *kanjeevaram* saree. Her thoughts went back to that fateful day.

She had entered matrimony; something she had never thought she would do in her lifetime. After having spent her entire childhood and adolescence in an orphanage, she had studied with a single-minded purpose. Determined to make a success of her academic career, she had completed her post-graduation and her Ph.D. early in life. At thirty, she was a doctorate in Biochemistry and worked as a post-graduate lecturer. Her life was filled with students, laboratories, experiments, research proposals and deadlines. She had met Hemant during a prize distribution function in college. She was compering a programme at the behest of her Principal and he had been invited as the chief guest. They interacted over tea, before and after the event. The Principal wanted him to inaugurate the Entrepreneurship Development Cell of the college and share his experiences with the students. He had charmed them all with his humorous banter and swept Prerna off her feet.

He, too, had been smitten by her and after a whirlwind courtship, they decided to tie the knot. It was just her colleagues and the Principal who formed the guest list from her side. On Hemant's side, there were a handful of his colleagues. All her dreams of ever being part of large, joint family remained unfulfilled because Hemant had no one to call his own. He had lost his parents in a train accident and had been raised by his maternal uncle, who died of liver cirrhosis when Hemant was barely 20, bequeathing him the factory that he had set up. It was a sick unit that Hemant decided to sell and used the proceeds to set up a small rental office where he assembled parts bought from the wholesale market into devices that enabled Wi-Fi connectivity in homes that had none. He had nursed the business back to health and after ten years of dedicated effort, was doing pretty well for itself.

All through her educational career, marriage had never been a priority. It was always something that she had concluded, was not for the likes of her. She was a nerd, someone who was too academically inclined to ever enter into wedlock. But life had sprung a surprise on her. Happiness, however, seemed to elude her. As a companion, Hemant was a trophy she loved to parade around initially. Soon she realized that they had no common interests. He immersed himself in his business and she got busy with college. There had been no kids and after the initial romance had died down, it had become a relationship where both of them had resigned themselves to a compromise. It was not one that operated on a plane of civility or grace, however. There were frequent fireworks. Words were unceremoniously exchanged and blame games were played making it a rocky relationship that was now reduced to being a sham for display in public.

Her life was like a tin of asafoetida or *hing*, as it was popularly called in Hindi. Long after it was empty, it was fragrant enough for people to assume it still contained the stuff. She was rich, with a handsome husband, a successful career and a beautiful home. The only thing they didn't have was a child. But somehow,

Prerna did not regret it at all. She no longer wanted one with Hemant. There were days when she secretly thanked God for having prevented this. In the last year, she had discovered that it was possible to open her doors to her students and that gave her immense satisfaction. The house no longer seemed silent or barren. Three of her students were living as paying guests and she enjoyed their company in the evening. The day stretched out endlessly because Hemant was hardly ever there. He was either away on outstation business trips or out socializing late into the night.

Today, he was up early. He had a meeting to attend and was hunting for something when Prerna asked him, "I am making breakfast for myself. Will you join me today, Hemant?"

"Hmm? No. You go ahead. I have a meeting at 8 in the office today. Am already running late. There were some papers I had left on the table here. Cannot seem to find them…"

"Oh those… they are all right here. Here, in this file. They were scattered all over the place and…"

Even as Prerna uttered the words, Hemant strode across the room and shouted, "Who asked you to fiddle with my documents? Why do you do these things? Don't you dare touch my papers ever again! I will now have to rearrange the whole set. I don't know why I tolerate you in my life at all. Stick to your research papers and your books. Leave my documents alone! I rue the day I decided to marry you!" Hemant walked out of the room in a huff, almost running into the three girls who were standing just outside the door, within earshot, aghast at what they had just seen and heard.

Prerna stopped in her tracks. “Don’t you dare talk to me like that! Never take that tone with me. Remember, you are living in my house, a house that is in my name, a house I run like a tight ship, you live in it like a non-paying guest, you are worse than my students. You do not even pay for your upkeep. Consider yourself lucky that I do not throw you out. If you cannot earn respect by your behaviour at least don’t test my tolerance. I don’t have any patience left. Leave.”

Hemant returned her icy stare with a dumbfounded expression, then shrugged his shoulders casually and exited silently.

Saturday, 24th April

10:03 p.m.

Manpreet Kaur had just finished her dinner. As she cleared her kitchen, she looked disapprovingly at her daughter, Renu. This was not what she had in mind for her daughter at all. If the hefty matriarch had had her way, her daughter would be the mother of two adolescent kids by now. But it was not to be. Not only was her daughter against marriage as an institution, she was also an atheist. She would have nothing to do with the community service that Manpreet took so much interest in. If the mother was famous for her contribution to the local *Gurudwara* with her culinary talent during the *langar* and her devotion towards serving the faithful, her first born would not so much as step into the place of worship. Manpreet Kaur was embarrassed by her eldest's refusal to toe the line. The *jatni* felt helpless. She had been widowed at thirty-nine and ever since, Renu had taken over the decision making for the family. Her father, Tejinder Singh, had worked as a caterer with a small business that just about tided the family over. His abrupt death following a cardiac arrest had left Manpreet devastated.

Tejinder Singh had not fulfilled any of his promises. There were three children to be educated, married off and settled down. Renu was just eighteen when her father died of a cardiac arrest, Simran and Harminder still in school. How on earth would she manage everything single-handedly. Renu had shown amazing grit and determination. She had completed a beautician's course in the summer holidays and decided to take up a job. Dropping out of college was her decision and she took complete responsibility for it, not once did she accuse her mother for having put her in such a situation. Renu started working at Clara's spa and also freelanced with her clients to make some extra money.

As she drained the tall glass of delicious *lassi* her *beeji* had lovingly placed by her bedside, Renu reflected on the eventful day. She could not believe this was happening to their salon. It was not good for business. Word of the death inside the spa would soon get around and it would only be a matter of time before people started speculating about the safety standards of their salon. Why did Rosy Fernandes have to die at *Clara's* of all the places on earth?

Monday, 26th April

8:30 a.m.

As Talpade poured the egg mixture onto the *tawa*, he wondered whether this case would turn out to be a death due to natural causes. There was a lot of work left to do before he could rule out homicide. He must talk to the neighbours of the deceased woman, interrogate her family doctor and also her colleagues.

The post mortem report would reach them only in a day or two. There was no wound on her person, no evidence of struggle, no suggestion of any kind of assault. Rosy Fernandes was a regular client. A facial was hardly a life-threatening routine. Each one of the employees had already been interrogated. Inspector Talpade had left the police station only at 8 p.m. after the FIR was filed and all the employees' statements recorded on the sole personal computer in the police station. The staff had been told not to leave the city till otherwise instructed. To rule out the likelihood of a homicide, they would have to think of people with possible motives. The post mortem report would have to show something concrete for them to continue with the investigation. Talpade quickly got ready and headed straight for the police headquarters at Bandra. It was almost 10:30 a.m. when he entered the police station.

Minutes later, his colleague, Ashutosh Dubey, walked in, and asked him eagerly, “Hi Pramod! Any update on the Rosy Fernandes case? Have you made any headway yet?”

“Yes. I have found out that Ms. Rosy Fernandes used to work for *Advent Electronics* as a secretary to the CEO, Mr. Hemant Trivedi, until recently. She had resigned three months ago although none of the employees had anything other than praise for her work. I spoke to the receptionist over the phone this morning. The CEO refused to see us. However, I insisted and have taken an appointment this afternoon.”

“Good work, Pramod. Interrogate Mr. Trivedi and his staff. Let us see what the gentleman and his employees have to say. Any other leads?”

“Yes. I am also planning to question Renu, the lady who gave Ms. Rosy Fernandes her head massage that day, once again. I have a feeling she knows more than she has told us in her statement.”

“Good idea. We can recreate a minute to minute timeline of events as they occurred on the day of Rosy Fernandes’ death. Come, let’s put it all down in order on the whiteboard.” Even as his friend spoke, Inspector Talpade picked up a black marker from the table and started listing the events of 12th April:

10:45 a.m. Rosy Fernandes walks into the parlour.

11:00. a.m. Renu gives Rosy a head massage after leaving another client, a Mrs. Charusheela Datta, who has just had hair colour applied on her scanty mane, to relax on the adjacent chair.

12 noon. Rosy Fernandes visits the toilet.

12:10. p.m. Renu serves water and tea to Rosy Fernandes.

12:20 p.m. Akshara starts the facial after speaking to someone who is saved as "Bhaiyya" on her phone for thirteen minutes.

1:05 p.m. Akshara leaves the cabin to call Renu.

1:07 p.m. Renu enters the cabin with Clara and finds Rosy Fernandes lying crumpled on the floor, still wearing the disposable gown. Clara D'Souza alerts the doctor and the police.

"Ashutosh, are there any cameras inside the parlour?" wondered Inspector Talpade.

"No, none. Parlours and salons are very careful in order to protect the privacy of their clients," said Ashutosh Dubey.

"Very well. You follow up with the company the client worked for. We will see what they have to say. Also do meet the doctor who has been assigned the autopsy on Rosy Fernandes and discuss the report with him. Find out if Rosy Fernandes had any close family members or relatives who can give us more leads on her medical history."

"I have just applied for a warrant to search her residence. I am sure the search will be fruitful."

"Fine, Ashutosh. Be sharp and keep me posted about the developments in the evening."

12:30 p.m.

Inspector Pramod Talpade strode into Kamran Apartments, flat number 203, Perry Cross Road. He looked around intently at the D'Souza's living room. The décor was tasteful and elegant. The owner could hardly be termed a suspect in this case as such an incident would mean very bad publicity for the spa. This automatically ruled her out but the investigative rule book stated very clearly that no one was innocent unless proved otherwise. Although Clara was not going to put her own business in jeopardy by murdering her own clients, it was standard operating procedure to interrogate everyone connected with the crime.

"Good evening, ma'am," he greeted Mrs. Clara D'Souza. "I would like to ask you a few questions, if you don't mind. This might take a while."

"Sure, Inspector," Clara said, visibly flustered and tired. "Please come this way."

Even as she spoke, the officer noticed the calm dignity with which she conducted herself.

"Thank you, Ms. D'Souza. Please tell me a little bit about yourself. We need to do a background check on all those involved. I am sure you understand and will cooperate. It will make things easier and expedite matters. Can you please tell me everything possible about your family, when and how you established your spa?"

Even as Clara started answering his queries, the officer checked out the few photographs kept alongside the mantelpiece beside the traditional candlesticks and crucifix that were a mandatory part of every Catholic household. One of the photographs showed the two sisters Freida and Clara with Clara's husband, Joe D'Souza in the centre. The two sisters looked radically different from each other. Freida was taller, a lot more angular, with high cheekbones and a rather stern face while Clara had rounded arms, lovely skin and lustrous hair with a well maintained, petite, smiling figure.

"Of course, sir. I do understand and you will have my complete assistance in any matter pertinent to the case. I want it resolved as much as you do. I come from a Bandra based Catholic family and am married to Joe D'Souza, an accountant with Swan International, an IT company. I do not have any children. I started this spa in 2005 with some savings that my husband generously offered by way of capital. Joe believed in me and invested in it, making my dream a reality. By God's grace and as a result of all these years of hard work, my spa is doing very well and we were even considering opening another branch soon. We were actively considering renting out an outlet in Bandra East but now with all this going on, we might have to stall those plans." Clara D'Souza paused and sipped some water from a glass kept on her table. "Would you like some coffee or tea sir? I am sorry I didn't ask earlier."

I need to speak to three of your employees again, the beauticians, Akshara and Renu as well as Maria, your housekeeper, concerning the sequence of events on the day Rosy Fernandes was found dead in your salon. I will also need your presence to corroborate what they say," said sub-inspector Talpade.

"Of course. Please go ahead, sir. We are all willing to assist you in any way necessary. I will send for all of them. They stay nearby and can reach within half an hour. Would that suit you, officer?" asked Clara politely.

"Yes. Thank you," said Talpade.

Clara sent for her employees and they spent the next half hour making small talk as they waited for the three to arrive. Talpade gathered a lot of information about her upbringing and her family. Soon the three employees arrived at Clara's residence. They looked anxious, tense, and as Renu once again narrated the events as they had occurred that day, Inspector Talpade watched her expressions closely. She looked at him warily.

"Ms. Renu, in your earlier statement you had mentioned that after you finished with massaging Rosy Fernandes' head she asked for water and tea. So, can you say with certainty that this was the food last consumed by her before she was found dead? Did she walk normally towards the cabin after that or did you notice anything unusual in her manner after she had relieved herself? Also, did she complain of any pain or discomfort during the massage?"

"No sir. She did not complain of anything at all." Renu's voice was strong and confident. "She only wanted to relieve herself. After that, she had some water and a cup of tea. That was the last thing I saw her consume, after which, Akshara started her facial."

"Did you have any conversation with her during the head massage? Did she talk sensibly or do you recollect anything she said as being out of the ordinary or unusual? Was she saying or doing anything that seemed weird to you?" Talpade persisted.

"Not at all, sir. In fact, she was not in a mood to talk."

This time Talpade noticed no hesitation in Renu's manner and was convinced by her confident replies. He decided to quiz Akshara once more; she was the one who had last seen Rosy Fernandes alive.

Akshara was already mouse-like in appearance; now her worried face had a severe pinched look that made Talpade look at her even more curiously. This seemed to agitate the girl further and she became even more reticent. "Look here, Ms. Akshara. Please do not think we are accusing you of anything here. We only want to establish the facts of the case. I need to report all these details and therefore have a few questions. Answer them calmly and honestly. You have nothing to fear if you have done no wrong. Tell me, when you administer a facial to any client what exactly is the treatment adopted? What is the nature of each step of the treatment? Please be specific. We need every detail."

A little reassured by his manner, Akshara decided that the best course of action was to be frank about everything. She had nothing to hide anyway. She was feeling a bit guilty about having taken that phone call before beginning with the facial earlier but now she realized that no one was looking at her accusingly at all. In fact, they were all very gentle. Methodically, she explained the process involved in a facial, from the cleansing lotion being applied to the steam being administered. “Did you notice any convulsions or cramps during the administration of the steam?” Talpade asked her. “Did she complain of any tingling in her skin or her throat after she had consumed the tea and water? Did she pick at the bed while the steam was being given? Was she restless when the cleanser was applied, or did she become uncomfortable only when the steam was administered?”

“Initially, she was like any normal client. She was not restless at all, except during steam, when she started coughing, took her medicine, then her cough worsened so I ran to get help.” Akshara was overwhelmed by the pointed questions and began to feel anxious once again.

“Was there any vomiting or nausea that you observed in the room? Or any purging when you came into the cabin?”

“No, sir.” Akshara was teary-eyed at the thought of it all and Talpade knew that this was a dead end. He was not getting any new information out of her.

“Who is this Bhaiyya on your phone who you spoke to for thirteen minutes before beginning the facial?”

Between bouts of crying, Akshara blurted it all out. Her day had begun badly. Her mother was not keeping well and she was wracked by guilt and worry. She had set out of her home in a rush and was impatient to get to her sick mother. Her brother’s phone call had made her even more anxious. She waited for Rosy Fernandes to finish her tea. The young girl was a bit flustered as she recounted how her brother Akash had expressed anxiety over her mother's health.

By 2 p.m. Talpade had spoken to Clara, Akshara, Renu and Maria. All four of them confirmed their earlier statements. Akshara was the only one who had entered the cabin after Rosy Fernandes. This was turning out to be quite a puzzler, Talpade thought. He decided to discuss the developments with Ashutosh that evening after he had met the CEO of *Advent Electronics*.

Advent Electronics,
3:03 p.m.

The secretary announced Inspector Pramod Talpade into the office of her CEO, Mr. Hemant Trivedi and ushered him inside. After extending the mandatory courtesies, the aging owner of *Advent Electronics* asked him wearily, "Yes, inspector, what can I do for you?"

"Well, sir, this concerns an ex-employee of yours, Ms. Rosy Fernandes. We wanted to clarify a few things."

"Look here. What happened to Rosy Fernandes after she exited my company is no concern of mine. She has resigned and I want nothing more to do with her and her matters." The old man looked visibly agitated. Something was definitely going on here and Pramod Talpade was determined to get it out of this man.

"I am afraid you cannot just wash your hands off the affair so easily, sir. I want to know exactly why she left the company. She is dead and we are investigating the case. Every little detail is relevant and if you are not guilty of any crime, I do not see why you should hesitate to answer our queries."

"Ahem… certain matters are of a delicate and confidential nature and concern me personally. I have the right to keep my private life private, haven't I?" The old man was getting belligerent and Talpade knew that this was when he would need to threaten him with a visit to the police station. That trick always worked.

"Of course. This simply means that we would have to take you to the police station and ask you a few questions that you would be liable to answer. We assure you that the answers will be kept strictly confidential and we will respect your privacy. Any knowledge that you keep from the police department is tantamount to obstruction of justice. So, would you like the interrogation to happen in the police station, sir?"

Hemant Ashok Trivedi was sweating profusely. "Maybe, we should discuss this in a civil manner over a cup of coffee…?"

Mr. Trivedi's secretary, a demure looking lady, brought in a cup of coffee in the next few minutes and Talpade ordered her to hand over the appointments register. He asked the photographer to click pictures of the CEO's schedule of the last three months – ever since Rosy Fernandes tendered her resignation. After that was taken care of, he proceeded to interview the other staff one after another. It was past 5 pm when he headed back to the police station with Havaldar Shetty.

When he entered the police station, he found Ashutosh Dubey creating a folder on the pc, saving all the pictures clicked during the investigation of their latest case. "This case may turn out to be a homicide Ashutosh. Certain facts have come to light! The lady who died at the parlour, Rosy Fernandes, resigned from her post three months ago quite suddenly, it seems. No one knows why. Also, Hemant Trivedi, the CEO of *Advent Electronics*, became nervous as soon as I mentioned Rosy's name. Broke out into a cold sweat, did not want to discuss anything further concerning her. His behaviour is extremely suspicious and I am sure he will spill the beans if I interrogate him further." Talpade was feeling almost gleeful at the prospect of an intriguing case to solve.

"I like your enthusiasm, Pramod. But what proof do we have? If the old man decides to lawyer up, how are we going to prove anything? Do we have a written statement? No." Ashutosh Dubey was an efficient cameraman and an experienced member of the team. Inspector Talpade was a diligent officer, a hard worker and a taskmaster. He was not going to get complacent. But it would not do if they conjectured without proof. "We need hard evidence, Pramod. Not just theories."

Pramod Talpade was in his early thirties. He respected his colleague for his experience and although Dubey was older, they had a great rapport and called each other by their first names. "I will get there, Ashutosh. I had given the flask that we recovered from Rosy Fernandes' handbag to the forensic department and I want you to talk to her family doctor to get to know her medical history. I am sure you will return with definite evidence. I also need a warrant to search Rosy Fernandes' apartment and phone records." Talpade was all fired up and excited by now.

Ashutosh smiled and said, "Please action the paperwork for the warrant. I will visit the forensic lab tomorrow and speak to the doctor in the morning regarding the post mortem. The warrant should be issued in a day's time. Good job, Pramod!" The cameraman liked this youngster's enthusiasm but he realized he would have to temper it from time to time without bruising his ego. After all, though young, he was his senior officer and he was expected to report to him.

The young inspector smiled gratefully "Thanks Ashutosh!"

Tuesday, 27th April

Lecture Hall 8C in RB College, Bandra, 11:30 a.m.

"Thus, we can see that there is an urgent need to develop culture collections of endophytic microbes. You can start working on your assignments as discussed. We will take them up in my next practical session on Wednesday afternoon." With that, Professor Prerna took up her folders and walked out of the laboratory. A young girl followed her into the staff room.

"That was an interesting session, Professor."

Professor Prerna turned to see which one of her students had complimented her. Her M. Sc. final year class was filing out in groups discussing the assignment she had just given them. As the classroom emptied, she noticed that a wiry looking girl dressed simply in a plain white kurti and blue jeans was standing behind her holding her journal.

"I would like to have a word with you, madam," said the girl. The professor was tired but the student seemed polite and sincere. So she relented, "Just give me a few minutes and then you can see me in my cabin."

Professor Prerna's cabin was a neat and uncluttered place. There was a glass cabinet with books on Biochemistry, Microbiology and Biotechnology stacked neatly with their spines and titles clearly visible. As she waited patiently, the girl surveyed the room and its decor carefully. A *warli* painting on the wall depicted a family gathering of some sort.

After she had placed her portable microphone, whiteboard marker and duster in her locker, the professor reached for the stainless-steel bottle on the right of her table and drained it of its contents with a sigh of satisfaction only drinking water could produce. Conducting practical sessions with a mask on constantly was a trial and it had tired her out. “Yes, tell me. What do you want? Are you a Masters’ student in my class? I don’t remember having seen you in my class before.” With a slightly apologetic nod the girl replied, “Yes, Madam. My name is Tanya Mishra.”

“I see. Go on.” said the professor.

The girl hesitated and then continued, “I have recently moved to Mumbai. My parents stay in Jharkhand. I work at a call centre in order to support them and I have been unsuccessful in finding any accommodation in the city that is affordable.”

Prerna raised an eyebrow, “What makes you think I can help?”

“Well, ma’am, I heard from some seniors that you have some research students staying at your place as paying guests and was wondering if you have space for one more. I would be much obliged madam.” The girl blurted out.

The lecturer took a moment before she answered the earnest girl. "I do appreciate the efforts you are putting in to support your family financially and do your post-graduation simultaneously. I don't know how I haven't noticed you in class earlier. However, I am afraid I already have a full house with three students living in my apartment as paying guests. Of course, I am not doing it for any financial reasons. One of them is a research student pursuing a Ph.D. under me and the other two are her friends. I only agreed to help her out till she was financially capable of renting out her own apartment. Sorry dear, but I really cannot help you."

The girl looked disappointed, but her voice was calm and gracious, "I understand, ma'am. It's okay. Thank you for your time."

Bandra West, Police Station
4 p.m.

The post mortem report was lying on the table and Ashutosh Dubey was in deep thought when Inspector Talpade entered the station. "What is the matter? Are there any new leads in the case?" The Inspector held the report up and skimmed over its contents:

PM No. 432/18

Body no. 3

Memorandum of a Post Mortem Examination held at CNGC Hospital Bandra

On the dead body of: Rosy Fernandes

Place: Bandra by Dr. Milind Phadnavis

General Particulars:

1. (a) By whom was the corpse sent? Inspector Pramod Talpade (Bandra Police Station)

   (b) Name of the place from which sent. Bandra, Mumbai.

2. By whom was the corpse brought and identified? Constable Sachin Shetty (B.No. 3678) (Bandra Police Station)
3. The date, hour and minute of its receipt: 24th April 2021, 4:30 p.m.

   (a)The date, hour and minute of beginning post-mortem examination: 24th April 2021, 5:30 p.m.

   (b) The date, hour and minute of ending post-mortem examination: 24th April 2021, 6:48 p.m.

4. Substance of accompanying report from police officer or magistrate, together with the date of death, if known and the supposed cause of death or reason for examination: As per the police inquest, the deceased was found dead at Clara's Spa at Bandra after a facial.

Probable age: 32 years

Height: 5 feet 3 inches

Probable time since death: The body was discovered within a few minutes of death at 12:30 p.m.

External Examination revealed the following:

The condition of the body: Rigor mortis had set in by the time the body was examined externally. It was almost 6 hours after death had occurred. There was no evidence of emaciation in the musculature as the body was that of a considerably young person.

Marks of identification: A mole behind her right ear.

The state of the natural orifices, eyes, ears, nostrils, mouth, anus, urethra and vagina were found to be commensurate with that of a normal female 32 years of age. A certain amount of redness was detected around the inner layer of the nostrils and the skin.

An examination of the genitalia and breasts reveal that the female had experience of sexual intercourse but had not delivered any foetus.

Additional remarks: The mouth had evidence of some salivation which signals some nausea prior to the occurrence of death.

Internal examination of the head, neck, scalp, skull, vertebrae, spinal cord, the peritoneal cavity, oesophagus, spleen, pancreas, bladder and kidneys reveal nothing out of the ordinary. A healthy bone structure is evident with no degeneration or injury of any kind.

The liver, however, indicates some scarring that is suggestive of poisoning.

The rib cage, pericardium, and diaphragm indicate no abnormality. An examination of the right and left lung revealed normal weight and size in keeping with the woman's age and structure.

The examination of the abdomen indicates that the woman had consumed alcohol prior to the occurrence of death. The contents of the stomach indicate that the deceased had consumed boiled egg and buttered white bread, tea and alcohol a few hours before death occurred.

The viscera and samples of materials collected from the body have been preserved as per the regulations using common salt, 40% formalin as fixative.

Blood samples have been topped with liquid paraffin in order to preserve them as the possibility of the death having occurred due to inhalation of irrespirable gases cannot be ruled out conclusively.

Opinion as to the cause of death: Traces of ricin have been found in the respiratory tract along with asthalin. Respiratory failure leading to cardiac arrhythmia can be concluded as having caused the death from the condition of the inner layer of the nostrils, lungs and respiratory tract. The inhaler and capsules of asthalin that were sent for examination with the dead body reveal the presence of ricin. Therefore, it can be concluded definitively that a lethal dose of ricin poisoning has caused the death. This is corroborated by the scarring found in the liver and the respiratory tract.

Inspector Talpade took stock of the case for a few minutes as he finished reading the post mortem report and then asked his colleague, "Ashutosh, what do you think of Renu's statement? She usually takes on the hair styling clients. Isn't it possible that she left her client after administering the head massage, for a few minutes? Get the contact numbers of that client and check with her personally if she left them even for a few minutes and at what time. Also do a background check on each one of Clara's employees and Clara herself. We cannot afford to miss out on anything.

The cause of death has been identified as a respiratory failure caused by ricin. It's a case of poisoning. The case now seems to be a homicide. I will visit Rosy Fernandes' residence and find out details about her GP. You can check whether Rosy Fernandes had any history of cardiac trouble, asthma, or issues with her blood pressure to ascertain whether there was something about her medical history that could have been aggravated by the ricin in the capsules."

Ashutosh looked up from his paperwork to say, "We have already taken the employees' statements, Pramod, but I have not checked with each one's clients. I'll get cracking on those. I have also asked Havaldar Sachin Shetty to tail Hemant Trivedi and monitor his movements closely. He will keep me informed about any developments at that end."

"Hmm. Good." said Inspector Talpade as he went back to his file thoughtfully.

Ashutosh Dubey checked Talpade's notes to see the names of the clients listed under Renu in order to verify who had occupied the chair adjacent to Rosy's during her head massage. He found one name and dialled her number. She responded immediately.

Mrs. Charusheela Datta, who had her hair coloured by Renu, arrived at the police station in less than an hour. She almost sailed in, wearing a bright chiffon sari printed with flowers in every possible hue with a sunny orange sleeveless blouse that made the fat around her upper arms dangle and jiggle like steamed eggplants. Yes, Renu had left her side after applying hair colour. Perhaps it was for around twenty minutes or so. She did not exactly remember the time but she did recall that it was when *We are all Foodies*, a cooking show was being aired on the television placed in the parlour. She had avidly followed the recipe for a *malai kofta* without garlic and onion and did not notice how time flew by. Even as Inspector Talpade listened attentively to the conversation between the lady and Ashutosh, he checked the show's timing and found that its telecast time was between 11:00 a.m. and 12 noon. That ruled out Renu. All of a sudden, another thought struck him. The post mortem report clearly mentioned ricin poisoning as the cause of death. Someone had mixed ricin in the capsules she used with her inhaler and those capsules were already in her handbag. It could not have been the employees in the parlour. It had to be someone else.

The Office of the Medical Examiner, Dr. Milind Phadnavis

4:30 p.m.

Dr. Phadnavis was about to take a tea break when Ashutosh Dubey walked in. The doctor insisted that the cameraman join him. He had neatly laid out a plate of biscuits along with hot tea that he poured meticulously into both their cups. As he bent over to pour some milk into the tea, he asked Ashutosh Dubey, "How much sugar would you like, officer?"

"Just one spoon. Thank you, sir. I have gone over the post mortem report and have a few questions. So, what kind of a poison is ricin, Dr. Phadnavis?"

"Do have some biscuits with the tea," said the doctor, offering the plate of glucose biscuits to his guest. He helped himself to a biscuit, then settled down to answer Ashutosh's questions. "Ricin is a protein toxin that has caused death due to poisoning in this case. It had to be a lethal dose that was inhaled by the victim along with the asthalin in the capsules. The cause of death has been identified as cardiac arrhythmia and respiratory failure. You could perhaps get hold of the deceased's medical history. It might prove to be helpful."

"That's a good suggestion, doctor. I will do that. Is there anything else that you observed and wasn't mandatorily mentioned in the report perhaps? Anything at all?"

"Well, the condition of her skin does not indicate any allergy to any cosmetic or substance which had been used on her during her visit to the spa either. The victim is quite young and her organs show no deterioration that is common with age, to have caused these symptoms. Nothing new to add other than what is already mentioned in the report. Another clarification I wish to make is that I don't think ricin was *mixed* with asthalin in those capsules. Those capsules *only* contained ricin. I have not found any trace of asthalin or any other substance other than ricin in them. Saying anything else would be guess work not supported by facts and I do not make conjectures." Ashutosh was taken aback and as he rose to help the medical examiner with the plate containing the biscuits and the cups of tea, made a mental note of this important revelation. Someone had replaced the asthalin capsules in the bottle with capsules containing ricin. Someone who was deft enough to do such an exercise. Was Hemant Trivedi, an aging man, capable of this, he wondered…or did he have an accomplice?

The conversation with Dr. Phadnavis had steered the investigation in another direction. There was a lot to work on now. Ashutosh thanked the doctor and left, eager to share his findings with Inspector Talpade. As he went past the busy pavement, an idea struck him. He immediately dialled the medical investigator's office and explained the matter to Dr. Phadnavis. He would have to make a special request and ask for the results as quickly as possible. After receiving an assurance that it would be done by the next day, he went back to the police station to wrap up all the paper work that had piled up.

This could turn the investigation in a completely different direction. It might even give it closure. There might be fingerprints on the capsules or the bottle containing them. If someone had deliberately poisoned the lady, they would have had some knowledge of her susceptibility to asthmatic attacks and the fact that she used an inhaler during such emergencies. The capsules containing ricin might have therefore been switched with the ones containing the asthalin. However carefully the murderer might have worked, it was possible that some fingerprints had been left behind. Adding the poison inside every capsule was tricky business. It had to be someone with a steady hand. How had he not thought of this angle before? Every case was teaching him how his focus had to become sharper and how much more attentive he needed to be. He quickened his pace, eager to share these findings with Inspector Talpade. But when he called him, there was no answer. He decided to head home. The update could wait. It was best to discuss this in person the next day at the police station.

Wednesday, 28th April

10 a.m.

The warrant for searching the victim's residence as well as the keys to her flat in hand, Talpade set off with Havaldar Shetty for 5, Perry Cross Road, Bandra – Rosy Fernandes' house as per the address in her bank passbook.

The apartment was neat and tidy. The living room had some indoor plants, paintings and handicrafts from different parts of the country and the décor was tastefully done. A well-equipped kitchen and a well-stocked refrigerator bore testimony to the fact that Rosy Fernandes frequently entertained guests. There were two glasses and two plates in the sink. Only one of the glasses had a lipstick stain. There were cigarette stubs in the ashtray.

Talpade and Shetty searched the mattress, pillows and storage spaces thoroughly. As Talpade approached the cabinet where Rosy Fernandes had hung her clothes systematically on individual hangars, he spied a small locker behind them. Using the smallest one of the keys in the set he had found in her handbag, he was able to open the safe. There was some jewellery, her passport and some cash. He shut the locker carefully and again looked around the living room. There was no evidence to suggest that Rosy Fernandes lived with anyone else. All the clothes and shoes he found seemed to belong to her. They were all the same size.

Talpade rang the neighbour's bell and a young Parsi girl answered the door. After interrogating the girl and her aged mother, he found that Rosy Fernandes was a spinster and lived on rent in an apartment owned by the widow of the late Pesi Shroff. The Parsi family had rented the flat out to her on a two-year lease. She was good tenant and paid her rent regularly and on time. "How did she pay them the rent?" Talpade asked. "Cheque or cash?" The old lady thought for a time, then said, "Well, now that you mention it, she usually paid by cheque. However, from January to March, she has been giving us cash for some reason. We were quite happy with the cash, of course." Talpade made a careful note of the fact, secretly thinking that the old lady had a tremendous memory. Taking advantage of this, he also enquired who their family doctor was and whether Rosy Fernandes also visited the same doctor. The lady replied in the affirmative. Talpade jotted down the name and number of the physician.

Rosy Fernandes was apparently friendly enough to exchange cookies and cakes whenever she baked any and the Parsi family also shared their traditional dishes with her. She did have friends over occasionally but they did not seem to know or remember anyone in particular. The young Parsi girl and her mother were quite distraught to learn that she had died. They could not, however, imagine that anyone would want to murder her.

Talpade went back into Rosy Fernandes' flat. He decided to do a thorough search to ensure he had not overlooked anything. As he looked around the place, he saw the traditional altar with Christ on the crucifix. It was an imposing marble figurine. He stood riveted for a while, staring at the image and the attention to detail evidenced in the sculptor's art. The bloodied hands and legs nailed to the crucifix as well as the crown of thorns on Christ's head looked realistic. He looked around the altar for a chest or box of some kind that could be used to store something valuable secretly but did not find anything. He was just about to move away when his fingers brushed against something under the candle stand that seemed to give way with the friction. He bent to see what he'd dislodged. A pen drive with a bit of cellophane tape stuck to it! What was so important in this pen drive that the dead woman had kept it taped secretly to the candle stand near her altar?

Talpade put the pen drive in his pocket.

Bandra West, Police Station

11:14 a.m.

When cameraman Ashutosh Dubey entered the police station, he found his Inspector Pramod Talpade staring intently at videos of young girls in a state of undress, pouting in front of a mirror. "What are you doing on duty, young man? Watching cheap porn? That too in a police station!"

Inspector Pramod Talpade stood up with a start and looked guiltily at his much older colleague. Embarrassed and red-faced, he blurted, “What!!? No! no! I was just checking the contents of a pen drive that I found at Rosy Fernandes’ flat, Ashutosh.”

“Yes, yes, by all means go back to the videos, investigate all you want. Let me not stand in the way of your thrills! I’ll go to my boring paper work on some other cases.” Guffawing with laughter, Ashutosh Dubey lumbered towards his desk, leaving a sheepish looking Talpade to his task.

“Relax, Pramod! I was just joking.” The cameraman grinned. “Jokes apart, what does this pen drive contain?”

Thrown off by the allegation, Talpade continued to stammer. “Arre, I have no idea. This case is getting quite curious. The Fernandes woman had been paying her rent in cash for about a year and had plenty more in her possession. She seems to have been involved in something underhand. We’ll have to investigate this further. What is the update from your end?” He was eager to change the topic and shut down the laptop. Ashutosh briefed his senior about all the medical examiner’s findings as well as his theory. The inspector agreed with his speculations and wanted him to follow up with Rosy’s family doctor as soon as possible.

Still laughing internally at the poor inspector’s expression, Ashutosh Dubey started leafing through his notes, trying to ascertain the contact information of Rosy Fernandes’ family doctor. He vaguely recollected him saying that he had jotted the name and number down somewhere. “Ah, there it was! Dr. Niharika Kulkarni,

MBBS." He dialled the number and luckily got an immediate appointment.

Dr. Kulkarni's clinic

1:30 p.m.

When the compounder indicated that he could go in, Ashutosh went in expecting to see a medical practitioner who was in her fifties, but he was surprised to find a pretty, cheerful and enthusiastic woman in her late thirties. Dr. Kulkarni had a broad forehead and an aquiline nose and was wearing an ethnic *salwar kameez* with bold block prints of the Buddha all over in maroon against an off-white border.

"Yes, officer. What can I do for you?"

"I was looking for some information on one of your patients. A Ms. Rosy Fernandes," said Ashutosh Dubey.

The doctor's eyebrows immediately shot up. "What has happened to her?"

"Doctor, she died suddenly during a facial. It seems she was uncomfortable when the steamer was turned on and started using her inhaler. However, it did not relieve her discomfort and she died on the spot. We are investigating her medical history, so any information that you could give us would be most helpful."

"Oh, my goodness! This is shocking. Unbelievable! She was not a chronic asthmatic at all. She only had occasional bouts of wheezing, purely allergic in nature, especially to air conditioners that had not been serviced in her office. Otherwise, she was quite hale and hearty.

Ever since I prescribed an inhaler to her, the incidences and her visits had also become few and far between."

"Let me just confirm this. Sushma, get me this patient's records. Ms. Rosy Fernandes." The assistant was prompt and soon the doctor was intently consulting her notes on Rosy Fernandes. "A patient's case history is always confidential…but I guess I will have to make an exception here. As far as I can see, for the last nine months or so there has been no bout of breathlessness at all. I cannot understand how she could have died so suddenly. If you don't mind, can you answer a few of my questions? I will be able to understand the case better then."

"Sure, doctor. Anything to help the case." Ashutosh replied, only too glad to be of assistance.

"What exactly was the visit to the beauty parlour for? I am just trying to rule out a couple of reasons that I can think of as a trigger for an asthmatic attack."

"Well, it was for a facial, head massage and hair wash. Nothing else. However, after the first few minutes of the facial, when the steam was being administered to her face, she started coughing uncontrollably and apparently reached for her inhaler. The inhaler did not help. In fact, according to one of the employees of the spa, it worsened the situation and she eventually collapsed. The doctor who was called found her dead." Dubey replied, looking at the doctor intently.

"Oh, so it was not for a hair colour or a bleach. Those two things could have triggered an asthmatic attack as the strong smell of the chemical is known to cause wheezing in some patients. But here, that does not seem to be the case. Another thing that I find strange is your report that her condition worsened after she inhaled asthalin. That is impossible. Asthalin should have relaxed her instantly instead of causing her death. Have you sent the asthalin and the inhaler for testing yet? Was it expired or something? That could be one of the reasons for making the inhaler ineffectual, especially if she has not had a bout in a while. The medicine might have lost its potency," said the doctor, thoughtfully.

"You certainly have a point there, doctor but let me clarify this. The capsules in her possession did not contain asthalin. Someone was trying to poison her. The forensic evaluation has detected ricin in the capsules. This is turning out to be a homicide and therefore, we may trouble you if we have any further questions." Ashutosh rose to take his leave. He enjoyed doing the spade work for Inspector Talpade. That was what made the job challenging. Otherwise, just clicking pictures of dead bodies and accident sites was mundane work.

"Sure officer. Anytime. This is my phone number. Even if I am with other patients, just text me and I will not keep you waiting. I am so taken aback by all this. Do let me know if I can help in any way." With these words, the doctor signalled to her compounder and assistant that the next patient could be sent in.

7 p.m.

Inspector Pramod Talpade was immersed in thoughts of the Rosy Fernandes case when he left from the police station that day. He took a sharp turn at the corner and almost knocked a girl standing at the bus stop. The girl was lanky and had short wavy hair. She was clad in blue denim and a light blue top and drummed her fingers impatiently against her cell phone. She seemed to be waiting for an auto. Talpade screeched to a halt very close to her, startling her with the suddenness of the act. The girl was about to give him a piece of her mind, as he extracted his head from the helmet. "*Baap re*! I don't believe this! Pramod!" She grinned and engulfed her college buddy in a bear hug. Talpade looked a tad embarrassed at this unchecked display of affection in a public place and smiled sheepishly at her. "Laasya! How have you been? It's ages since we met. What are you doing currently? Where are you working?"

"Oh… ho… hold it, Officer Talpade! One question at a time. This is not one of your police interrogations. Why don't you give me a lift to the station and we can catch up on all the news en route? I am running a bit behind schedule."

Laasya updated Pramod during the ride on how she had gone on to take up a medical investigator's job in the US for almost a decade and had enjoyed the experience of assisting in police investigations. She had been forced to quit the job as her aged parents were unable to cope with their failing health. She wanted to be there for them and had therefore decided to set up her own practice as a private investigator in Mumbai. Till she raised enough capital to set up such an establishment, she would work as a biotechnologist in one of the larger well-paying pharma companies. Her younger brother was still studying law and she was excited at the prospect of a start-up of this kind in her hometown.

Pramod stopped his bike outside the railway station, glanced at Laasya's fit body approvingly and said, "*Ekdum fit hai tu*! Have you married at all?"

"No wedding bells for me, Pramod. I don't intend to fall into that trap, ever. This is indeed a happy coincidence, meeting you like this. I could use some advice on how to go about setting up my own detective agency here in Mumbai. What about you? How many kids do you have?"

Pramod Talpade frowned, "What makes you think I have kids? I am not even married!" he exclaimed, rather affronted by her assumption.

Laasya smiled and punching him in the shoulder declared, "*Dil pe mat le yaar*! Just kidding! Listen, why don't we meet up for dinner tomorrow? Just like old times, in that restaurant near our college? Would you like that?"

Appeased by her peace offering, Talpade grinned and said, "I am stationed at Bandra Police Station. Yes. That would be a good idea and we can talk at leisure! Shall I pick you up from your residence at eight or would you prefer to meet me there directly?"

"Will meet you there directly, Pramod! *Chal*, my train is due any minute. See you at eight!" With that quick response and another bear hug, Laasya sprinted across the flight of steps leading to the foot overbridge. Pramod watched her lithe form spring into the general compartment of an Andheri bound local train with an agility that he could only admire.

Now here was a girl after his heart. This was a friendship he had sincerely enjoyed. One could not call it platonic or romantic. He could bare his heart to her without fear of being judged or being given hypocritical replies. He never had to worry about being chivalrous when he was around with her. They had been study buddies initially and then had also bonded over camp during NCC, where Laasya had mastered rifle shooting and rappelling faster than him. It was Laasya who had taught him both. The bonfire night where they had sung old Bollywood songs and danced with the other cadets without a care about how they looked or sounded had thawed his rather rigid personality to warmth that he had somehow never achieved around any other friend. He was glad to have her back in his life.

He would hear her out and then dissuade her from this weird and highly impractical start-up idea that she had got into her head. The forensic department could definitely use her services. He resolved mentally that he would ask her to mail him her resumé and put in a word with Dr. Phadnavis. Her experience abroad would prove invaluable to their cases and they could become a superb team. Looking forward to a productive partnership, Pramod Talpade revved his bike and drove away with a smug expression on his handsome face.

7:45 p.m.

A jet-black duffle bag slung over his shoulder, Inspector Pramod Talpade dismounted from his bike and carefully strapped his helmet to the seat, snapping its clasp in place. He was in plain clothes. He didn't want unnecessary attention over his visit to the Trivedi household. As it is, he knew that the old man would not appreciate the intrusion. He had, however, shown enough foresight to get a search warrant for both residences - Rosy Fernandes' home and the Trivedi home because he knew that the senior citizen would try to prevent a thorough search of the flat.

He surveyed the colony carefully. A plush housing society with a beautifully maintained garden in the centre; the play area filled with the happy squeals of children enjoying their time with their friends and mothers on the merry-go-round, monkey bars, see-saw and the swings. The colourful paint on the mushrooms, giant beetles, butterflies and frogs made the garden an attractive sight for anyone who entered the complex. Another thing that the officer noticed instantly was that the place was breezy and well ventilated, something that was unique in Mumbai city. As he scrutinized the area around the housing colony, he noticed that it was parallel to the sea side and therefore blessed by the wind Gods. The garden was surrounded by twelve buildings named after the twelve Greek Olympian Gods – Zeus, Poseidon, Hades, Ares, Apollo, Hephaestus, Hermes, Hera, Aphrodite, Artemis, Demeter and Athena.

He checked with the watchmen downstairs and was directed to Athena, flat numbers 703 and 704. As he took the lift to the Trivedi residence, the officer could not help but think of his chance meeting with Laasya last evening. It would be nice to have a friend he could discuss his cases with after working hours. He badly needed someone's company without it impinging on his time and space in a way a relationship or a marriage would.

Flat numbers 703 and 704 were adjacent to each other and even before he had entered them, he could get a sense of its inhabitants' personalities. The doorway had a fancy teak board embossed with golden lettering saying *Trivedis*. There were aesthetic looking artefacts and a typically Keralite *uruli* with marigolds and roses floating on it with a candle in the centre. Only an affluent individual could afford to maintain these appearances. Very indulgent, reeking of an egoism that was trying really hard to project a cultural ethos. The lifestyle of the elite, he thought as he rang the doorbell. He had to ring it twice before the door finally opened.

A dignified looking lady in a crisp cotton sari walked into the living room. She had an imposing personality, with short shoulder length hair, a big *bindi* and ethnic silver jewellery that was simple yet elegant. She wore nothing around her neck, but Talpade could not help staring at the chic design on her ring. It was unique. Like a serpent coiled around an anchor. Her bare arms were slim and her nails carefully manicured. Noticing the greying hair around her temples and the marks on either side of the bridge on her nose, Talpade concluded that she was used to wearing glasses, for reading at least. He rose and extended his hand to introduce himself. She seemed slightly taken aback when he identified himself as a sub-inspector in plainclothes and identified herself as Mrs. Prerna Trivedi.

The fact that the old man had such an elegant looking wife was a bit of a shock to him. She must be around sixty, but she was fit and sophisticated. The manner in which she communicated and conducted herself was impressive. It took conscious effort on Talpade's part to tear his eyes away from her graceful form, fingers and manner. A captivating woman indeed. As soon as he started asking her a question or two, she interrupted him and asked for his identification. He gave her his ID card and also the search warrant.

Raising an eyebrow, she enquired, "Is there anything particular you are looking for, officer? My husband is a businessman, a family man. He is hardly a criminal. What do you suspect him of? What kind of circumstance has necessitated a search warrant of his residence?" All this was asked in an even tone, in a crisp manner, without raising her voice or losing her temper.

"Madam, I am sorry for this intrusion into your home. However, in order to aid our investigation, it is necessary that I search your husband's office and home. I would request you to kindly cooperate with the law. A woman, who was until recently his employee, has been found dead under mysterious circumstances. We would like to investigate the matter further as we have found some incriminating evidence of a confidential nature that I am not at liberty to disclose at present. Please understand that I am here in an official capacity and will do everything in my power to be discreet about my enquiry. Kindly conduct me to your husband's room so that I can search the place." Talpade was polite but firm.

Mrs. Trivedi grimaced. She looked clearly displeased and was about to reach for her cell phone, when three adolescent girls wearing smart kurtis and jeans, walked in. All of them were extremely pretty. Mrs. Trivedi stiffened. "Go inside your room, all of you. Now!" Her voice was suddenly curt, almost harsh.

The girls looked familiar to Talpade. Where had he seen them recently? He tried his best to recollect but he was unsuccessful. He decided to investigate further. He quizzed Prerna Trivedi about the girls, not wanting to let this moment pass without seeking a clarification. "Your daughters, ma'am?"

She was clearly disturbed by their appearance. "No. We do not have any children. They are my paying guests. Actually, one of them is my student and the other two are her friends. I allow them boarding and lodging here as a personal favour to my student, not that we need the money or anything. I do not want them to get a whiff of what's going on, officer. Please, you promised me that you would be discreet. What is going on? I have a right to know. Who has been found dead? What has my husband got to do with it? He is an innocent man. He has not killed her, I am sure." She had begun to sound slightly hysterical.

It was natural for her, as a wife, to be agitated at the prospect of a policeman searching her home. Talpade waited patiently till she calmed down. Finally, Prerna Trivedi managed to gather her wits about her and let out a sigh of resignation. “Let’s get this over with. You are not going to find anything here, anyway. Come. Let me show you our bedroom and the study.”

He followed her on a guided tour of the twin flats. The house was neatly maintained. Both the living rooms of flat numbers 703 and 704 had been joined by demolishing the wall separating them. As a result, the hall was rather spacious. There was a 48-inch Home Theatre; curios from various countries were strategically and tastefully placed all over the room. The passage leading to the bedroom was lined with photographs of the couple on various holidays and there were also some pictures of Mrs. Trivedi with groups of students that suggested that she was probably a teacher.

They entered the study on the right-hand side and the sight that greeted him confirmed his suspicions. Row after row of books on various subjects – fiction, non-fiction, scientific texts and encyclopaedias systematically lined two huge bookshelves. Even as he glanced admiringly at the collection, he quickly opened the couple of drawers on the study table to check their contents. The laptop kept on the table piqued his interest. “That’s mine, not my husband’s. Do you want to check my belongings too? Am I part of this investigation?” She was slowly turning belligerent again. Talpade decided to lay off.

“No, madam. May I see your bedroom? Does your husband use a laptop at home?” He turned towards the bedroom even as he spoke. Prerna Trivedi was clearly uncomfortable at the sudden intrusion. She quickly covered some undergarments and lingerie lying scattered over a chair with a towel. "No. He usually keeps his laptop in his office. Why do you want his laptop? What is it you want? Please tell me. I have a right to know. I am his wife!"

Talpade knelt down to check the shelf at the bottom of the study table. Looking up at the rather frustrated lady staring at him, he stood up and said, "I am done here now, but I would need to interrogate your paying-guests and servants. Would you prefer that I ask them to come over to the station or shall I go ahead and ask my questions here?"

Prerna Trivedi wrung her hands. "Do whatever you have to. Make it quick." She marched him into the adjacent bedroom and knocked on the door.

"Girls, this is Inspector Pramod Talpade. He wants to ask you a few questions." She turned to him. "They are innocent girls who work hard for a living. They stay away from their families in order to provide for them and deserve their privacy. They have nothing to do with your case. But have it your way. I would much rather have you question them here than make them pay you a visit in the police station." She folded her arms in a defiant manner and stood guard over the girls as Pramod Talpade began his interrogation.

As soon as Talpade entered the girls' room, the videos flashed in front of his eyes. This was the same layout. The dressing table and the painting were the same. These were the girls whose videos he had seen on the pen drive that Rosy Fernandes had in her possession. He tried to visualize the backdrop of the room and attempted to figure out the placement of a hidden camera. His eyes scoured the room. He discovered a multiplug adapter that could contain a hidden camera providing the same video angle. He scrutinized it closely with gloved hands and decided to take it along as evidence. It would have to be dusted for fingerprints. “What is going on officer? Please tell me. Why are you taking away things from my house?” Prerna Trivedi was indignant. Inspector Talpade turned to Mrs. Trivedi and said, “Madam, I need to interrogate the girls. I want you to cooperate with this investigation. Please leave the room for a few minutes. If you don’t cooperate, I will be left with no choice but to call them to the police station for questions.”

Mrs. Trivedi looked unsure. She was about to protest when the girls signalled to her and said, “It’s o.k. ma’am. Don’t worry. We will be fine.” Reluctantly, a visibly disturbed Prerna Trivedi left the room, closing the door behind her. Inspector Talpade turned to the girls and in a reassuring voice said, “I am the officer investigating the possible murder of Rosy Fernandes, a former employee of *Advent Electronics*. Mr. Trivedi was her boss. I have a few questions to ask you girls. Please cooperate and do not hide any facts from me. I assure you that whatever you tell me will be treated as strictly confidential. I want you to tell me what your opinion of your teacher’s husband is. What kind of a man is he? Has he ever misbehaved with you in any way? Did you ever sense anything amiss?”

The girls exchanged glances and one of them said, “No sir. Uncle has never misbehaved with me. He minds his own business and in fact, is usually out of station on business related matters. He is very rarely at home."

"Hmm…fine. Tell me, how was his behaviour towards his wife?" Talpade prodded the girls who looked a little hesitant.

One of the girls looked confused. "They are an ordinary couple sir. Every married couple fights. They also have had their share of fights."

"Have you ever witnessed your teacher confront her husband or retaliate in any fashion?" he asked, patiently waiting for one of the girls to respond and give him something more to work on.

"No sir. Not to the best of my knowledge" said the older of the two girls.

"Listen girls. Please understand. This is an investigation that is ongoing and therefore I do not want you to leave the city without informing me. I may want to ask you some more questions and you might be asked to come to the police station for further enquiries. Is that clear?"

"Ok sir," said the girls, with worry writ large across their foreheads.

When Talpade walked out of the room, he found Prerna waiting just outside it.

She looked livid. "You owe me an explanation! What exactly are you doing? You cannot just barge in and interrogate these girls!" Talpade maintained a stoic silence and left with the words, "Madam, this is a police case. Your husband is a suspect in a case that involves the death of his ex-secretary Rosy Fernandes. Please do not leave the city without informing us. We may interrogate you once again soon."

Thursday, 29th April

10:30 a.m.

Dr. Phadnavis came out of his laboratory for a breath of fresh air and a cup of coffee. He sometimes wondered whether he had made the right choice when he signed up as Medical Investigator for the Maharashtra Government. It was after a lot of deliberation that he had opted for the world of the dead. The world of the living was too complicated for him to handle. At least here, there were definite answers. Inspector Talpade had just come in with fresh evidence that needed to be dusted for fingerprints. It was something that looked like a mobile phone charger but interestingly had a hidden camera inside. What gadgets were floating around in the market these days!

The fragrant brew was a welcome reprieve after all the formalin he had inhaled. He had worked through most of the night and was planning to take a well-deserved break. He often had his breakfast in his office and slept blissfully on the couch. The fan made a bit of a racket but it never bothered him. He was so fatigued after every post mortem examination. He preferred to work with his assistant, Prashant Mhatre, who would meticulously jot down everything he dictated and prepare his reports. However, Prashant had recently shifted to Nanded after his wedding. He had decided to work for a government hospital after having partnered with Dr. Phadnavis successfully for over seven years. The doctor missed him sorely. Prashant had been a good friend and an efficient co-worker. It was hard to find a good replacement in his line of work. His reverie was interrupted by the entry of a lady who barged in with an eighteen-year old boy in tow. “Aarti! What a pleasant surprise! What on earth are you and your son doing here?” Dr. Phadnavis was astounded to see his sister and nephew.

“Daada, only you can help me. I just landed in Mumbai today. My son has been asked to take up an internship project by his college and he is insisting that he will intern here. I did not discuss it over the phone as I was sure he would be rejected. Please dada. Give him a chance to intern here. I don’t see how any other hospital or organization will take him without any contacts or influence. I know this is a government establishment and everything here is confidential. He will keep it confidential too. He just wants to spend a few days here. He will ask you a few questions and prepare a report and leave as soon as his project is done. Please!” Aarti was a housewife and a single mother. She had lost her husband a couple of years after her marriage in a tragic accident and had single-handedly brought up her son braving all odds. He was interested in medicine and had cleared all his entrances with distinction. He was a reticent boy but bright. Dr. Phadnavis grimaced at the prospect of having to bend his knee in order to swing the necessary permissions. He did not like asking for favours. He would have to, for his sister and nephew’s sakes. There was no way he could say no to dear little sister and favourite nephew.

"Sure. Don't worry. I will take care of it. Come, why don't you sit down? Let me order something for you to eat." Secretly, Milind Phadnavis bid his power nap a silent goodbye and resigned himself to another tiresome day.

Amey had impressed Dr. Phadnavis with his zeal and curiosity during one of his earlier visits and so he did not mind helping him out. The boy had already joined him at his table. His task today was to examine the inhaler, the asthalin capsules and the charger with the hidden camera for fingerprints. As he proceeded to isolate the fingerprints, he watched his nephew curiously out of the corner of his eye. Amey never spoke unless spoken to, but he was intrigued by the activity and occasionally asked some pertinent questions. "Mama, why do these capsules look a little wrinkled? Aren't capsules usually smooth and shiny?"

"Yes, Amey. You are absolutely right. That is certainly suspicious. These capsules have been tampered with and I will now run tests on the covering of the capsules to determine whether there are any fingerprints and whether the fingerprints match the ones on the charger with the hidden camera in it."

Phadnavis worked relentlessly. At 3 p.m. he called the police station and asked for Talpade. "I have run the tests, Pramod but could not find any fingerprints on the capsules or the inhaler. Whoever has tampered with them to add ricin had a steady hand and had probably used gloves. I did however find prints on the charger and they match those of Mr. Hemant Trivedi's that you had submitted earlier."

Amey had been listening to the conversation intently. "What is ricin mama? Is it a chemical?" he asked.

Smiling at the lad, Dr. Phadnavis said, "Ricin is a very powerful protein toxin, Amey. It is particularly concentrated in the seeds of the castor plant. It is a poisonous powder that can act in a crystalline form as well as when dissolved in liquid. It can prove to be fatal to human beings in a lethal dose. The quantity that is present in these capsules has clearly been used in order to murder the intended victim and would have sufficed to do the job with one or two inhalations."

"Wow! This is so cool! You are actually helping unravel a murder. I would certainly like to work in an office such as this one. What courses would I have to do to become a medical investigator?"

"I will definitely tell you if you are interested but it will take a lot of hard work and patience."

3:36 p.m.

Having taken Hemant Trivedi's fingerprints during the visit to *Advent Electronics* had proved to be immensely useful when they tried to match them with the ones they found on the camera that looked like a charger. The fingerprints and the videos on the pen drive were sufficient to build a case against the old man.

The procedure to initiate all the paper work was tedious and it was close to tea time by the time it was done. Finally, he had the search warrant in his hands and he went in uniform to Hemant Trivedi's office along with constable Shetty. It was 4:45 p.m. by the time they reached *Advent Electronics*.

The staff was shocked to see the police. As the police searched the place, ransacking the contents of every drawer and shelf, Hemant Trivedi's accountant, Mrs. Sumitra Desai, hung around curiously to see what they were looking for. The constable finally called out to Talpade from Hemant Trivedi's cabin. "Sir, please come here."

When Talpade went across, he found the constable holding a small packet containing a whitish powder that had been stashed way inside a small pantry in his office. Meanwhile, unable to contain their curiosity, the staff approached the officer. "Is it drugs? Is that what the packet contains? Our boss and drugs! You must be mistaken, sir. I am sure this is a mistake. Someone must have planted it here sir."

Talpade turned around. "Who told you that the packet contains drugs? Have you planted it here? Does it belong to you? Does any of this concern you? Come aside for questioning. There are quite a few queries I have of you." Talpade let off a barrage of questions that he felt compelled to unleash at this busybody who was minding everyone else's business but his own. The man cringed and took three steps backwards. "Err… no one told me anything, sir. I was just guessing. I have never seen this packet here sir and I have nothing to do with all of this."

"O.k., tell me then Mr…?" Talpade looked at the middle-aged man quizzically.

"Atre. Shrikant Atre, sir. I am the manager here," The man was wary now. His demeanour had transformed completely. The last thing he wanted was trouble from the police. Everyone was suspected by the police. They trusted no one and questioned everyone as if they were all culprits. This was common knowledge.

The manager could visualise his wife badgering him for shooting his mouth off when he could very well have stayed silent and kept his precious thoughts to himself. He realized at that moment that the loyalty he felt towards his boss need not be demonstrated in front of the police. If, for some reason, the man was guilty of a drug related crime, he, Shrikant Atre, a pious, disciplined man, would allegedly become Hemant Trivedi's associate in crime and therefore a suspect from whom information could potentially be extracted. He had heard several horror stories about how the police treated witnesses whom they took to the police station for questioning. There was no saying what percentage of truth lay in those rumours, but why take any chances? It was best to stay mum.

Cursing himself for acting rashly, Mr. Atre slowed down and decided to retrace his steps using hospitality as his defence. "May I offer you some tea or coffee sir?" he enquired politely. Inspector Talpade was a seasoned police officer. He could read the tell-tale signs of a potential witness anywhere. "Sure. I could use a cup of tea and some biscuits, if you please. It will give me some time to talk to you. I would like to know more about your boss, Mr. Atre. What can you tell me about your CEO? Come, let's sit in Mr. Trivedi's cabin so that we can chat undisturbed. Shetty, don't send anyone inside here other than the person bearing the tea and biscuits. I do not want to be disturbed." Talpade sank into the comfortable chair that had, until recently, nestled the heavy butt of its CEO.

Mr. Shrikant Atre's anxiety mounted exponentially at the request. Distressed, he called out to his peon, Subhash, and asked him to bring tea and biscuits into the CEO's cabin. Restless and discomfited, he sat on the edge of the chair on the opposite side of the glass topped table staring fixedly at the police officer who, by now, was swaying from side to side in the revolving chair with what looked like a villainous expression.

The manager was now sweating profusely. As he mopped his brow in consternation, Talpade felt his phone vibrate for the third time. He decided to take the call. Three rings in quick succession in spite of no answer could mean two things. It was either someone in an emergency who had his number or the DIG. It was the DIG expecting an update on the latest case. "Yes sir. Pardon the delay in responding to your calls, sir. The phone was on silent mode and I was interrogating some new witnesses. There has been a development in the ricin poisoning case, sir." Pramod Talpade got onto the defensive mode rather quickly with his boss in spite of the fact that he was only doing his job and not expected to pick every call while on duty.

DIG Vinod Paradkar's voice boomed from the other end, "Calm down, Pramod. I only called because it was urgent. The Commissioner wants an update on all the unsolved cases in the past 48 hours as soon as possible. I have to report to him. So, tell me, what is the development?"

"Sir, we discovered a packet of some whitish substance stashed deep inside Hemant Trivedi's locker," Talpade reported in a hushed tone. "Yes, sir, err...certainly sir. I will keep you updated on all the developments. I am just interrogating the staff now."

He listened intently to the instructions given for the next four to five minutes, promised to get back as soon as the interrogation was over and keeping the phone back in his pocket, he turned his undivided attention to the man in front of him. Shrikant Atre was by now cringing with fear.

"So, Mr. Atre, what can you tell me about your boss?" Within a few minutes Talpade knew he had found a very useful witness. The man was capable of verbal diarrhoea. He went on and on about his employer. It seemed as if Mr. Trivedi could do no wrong. The fact that he was a suspect in the case was something he found quite difficult to believe.

"Sir, our boss is a man of principles. He has a heart of gold. I have never heard anyone speaking ill of him. He was always so helpful. Three of my daughters' weddings happened because the man gave me generous loans without charging any interest. He lent me money on a payable when able basis. Who does this in this time and age, sir? Why, his helpful nature extends beyond this office, sir. I used to deliver money personally to a lady every now and then to an address in Andheri. This lady was a person with a young daughter who went to school. Sir used to sponsor her education."

"I see. Thank you for this interesting information. Please give me the address of this place in Andheri. We would like to confirm what you are saying. Also, tell me what you remember about your employer's ex-secretary Ms. Rosy Fernandes. What were the circumstances under which she resigned her job? She seems to have been quite efficient at work. What made her resign?"

"I really don't know, sir. It must have been some personal matter. She was also treated in a very humanitarian manner by our boss. At her behest, she was given all her dues in cash. I am sure she was in some sort of trouble. The boss helped her also with a lot of money. It must have been a couple of lakhs at least. He was a do-gooder; a man who was always ready to help the needy. You are suspecting the wrong person sir."

Talpade said nothing and proffered a pen and paper for Atre to write down the lady's address. The man hastily scribbled down whatever he remembered of the address. Talpade decided that his next stop was going to be Andheri. This case was taking an unexpected turn. Perhaps his visit to this lady would lead to something more. He studied the paper that bore Atre's spidery scrawl. Pranali Dive, 305, Jeevan Dhara Apartments, Third floor, Mahakali Caves Road, Andheri West, Mumbai.

Talpade strode out of the CEO's office. Following his boss' instructions to send the packet containing the whitish powder across to the medical investigator's office for examination through Havaldar Shetty, he thought about what the manager had said. It would be necessary to ascertain some kind of a paper trail in order to issue an arrest warrant. The police would need proof. Things would move only when the medical investigator confirmed their suspicions. Even as he thought all this, he stopped in his tracks.

He mentally replayed the telephonic conversation with his boss. "Things are too neat and tidy in this case, Pramod," his boss had said. "A person who is guilty of a crime will not hang around and keep incriminating evidence in his locker. He will not invite police attention towards himself aware of the possibility that Rosy Fernandes might have a visiting card on her person linking her to *Advent Electronics*. After all, until very recently, she was an employee there. Let us assume for a minute that the whitish powder is Ricin and not anything else, would it not be too much of a coincidence that Ricin was discovered in the asthalin capsules, its traces were found on the inhaler itself and to top it all, a whole packet of the poison was discovered in Hemant Trivedi's own drawer in his office? If the man was guilty, would he have allowed all this to show up in the autopsy and knowingly left a bag of the stuff behind in his own office, fully aware that the police would come looking after establishing the connection between Rosy Fernandes and *Advent Electronics*? After all, she was an ex-employee. No one is going to get any prizes for making that connection! It does not take a genius to identify Hemant Trivedi as the culprit behind the death of Rosy Fernandes. If he was really responsible, he would not be waiting in his office like a sitting duck! Everything sounds too easy to be true. There is definitely something that we are missing here. There's an important piece of the jigsaw puzzle that we have to find before we put together the actual picture. Another thing, Pramod, the CEO of *Advent Electronics* is at least 65 years old. He might be a sick character mentally and disgusting in his lechery, but his hands would not be steady enough to fill ricin systematically in each of the capsules."

All the excitement that Talpade had felt a while ago fizzled out. It was not going to be easy to nab the culprit in this case, after all. This was going to take a while, but the old man had to be nailed for his intrusion into the unsuspecting paying guests' privacy. That much could definitely be ensured. Determined to put the unlawful senior citizen behind bars for this crime, Talpade walked out of the CEO's cabin. By now, his mind was racing with several thoughts calling for his attention all at once.

The DIG was right. Assuming that Hemant Trivedi did engineer the whole thing, how had he managed to replace the asthalin in the capsules with ricin? How had he managed to go anywhere near Rosy Fernandes after she had started blackmailing him? Wouldn't she have been on her guard whenever he was around? She would not have let him anywhere near her handbag. It was the first place anyone would think of looking while searching for a pen drive that contained the incriminating videos. This was all proving to be too much of a sitter!

As far as the police were concerned, they now had concrete evidence to arrest Hemant Trivedi. Talpade could not help thinking that the old man was a lecherous scum of the earth. There was no question about his being guilty of taking advantage of three innocent young girls. Who knew how many other such girls or employees he had been filming or photographing over the years? This was perhaps the first of his offences that was being unearthed. Maybe there were many more.

Curbing his temptation to unravel the modus operandi behind the premeditated murder of Rosy Fernandes, Talpade decided that for the moment, it would be judicious to take the man into custody, then let the law take its course. The trial would anyway, if there was going to be one, be at a later date. They would have sufficient time to work out how the crime had been committed and whose help had been solicited. As of now it did seem as if he had an accomplice. Was Shrikant Atre that accomplice? Privately resolving to discuss these thoughts with his Ashutosh or even better, Laasya, Talpade wiped the sweat trickling down his brow with a broad white handkerchief that had, by now, become a mute recipient of several brown streaks and looked upwards at the ceiling fan as if it would favour him by blowing some cool breeze in his direction. The Mumbai summer was punishing in its humidity.

Talpade forced himself to stay focused on the evidence that they had unearthed instead of questioning its reliability. The sixty-year old CEO of *Advent Electronics* deserved to be arrested under Section 66E of the Information and Technology Act. The evidence was there for all to see.

The pen drive, the suspicious powder discovered in his office and the post mortem report were all suggestive of a premeditated crime. The judge could not dispute or ignore all this evidence. That he had a clear motive had been established. What the police would now have to determine was the method behind the murder. Was there an accomplice? Would an old man dare run the risk of confiding in another human being and allow someone to have a hold over him and his reputation? Wasn't that why Rosy Fernandes was killed in the first place? Was someone in *Clara's Spa* connected to Hemant Trivedi? Was it one of the clients? Was it one of the employees at *Advent Electronics*? Who could it be? Who could have helped him out here?

As he walked out of the cabin, he noticed, for the third time, the accountant trying to approach him as if she wanted to talk to him but was afraid to do so in front of the rest of the staff. He wrote his number on a piece of paper and quietly thrust it in her hand on his way to the washroom, saying, "Call me if you have any information." The lady took the chit and disappeared into her office.

Talpade shrugged and busied himself thinking about the paper work in the Rosy Fernandes case. They could now arrest Hemant Trivedi as a suspect in a murder case. Trivedi had violated the privacy of three unsuspecting girls who were his paying guests. It was an abominable act but, unfortunately, he would be eligible for bail. If they could only nail the bugger on charges of murder, he would serve a life sentence. Preoccupied with these thoughts, he rushed to the medical investigator's office.

Dr. Milind Phadnavis did not disappoint. He was as efficient as ever. Talpade had also taken Laasya along to introduce her to him. She was excited to be there as the investigation reached its final stages. Dr. Phadnavis was impressed by her observations and so was Amey. As Laasya and Amey got talking, the medical investigator confirmed that the whitish powder was a pure form of Ricin.

The arrest warrant could now be initiated and the old man finally tried in a court of law for violating the privacy of his paying guests and for murdering Rosy Fernandes in cold blood. They finally had proof. Hemant Trivedi had a secret stash of ricin hidden inside his office. His fingerprints had also been found on the charger with the hidden camera. His ex-secretary had been blackmailing him after she had stumbled upon the videos of the girls who lived as paying guests at his residence. The old man was a lascivious and lecherous murderer. He had murdered his secretary in cold blood. What now remained was to interrogate him about how exactly he had poisoned Rosy Fernandes. What was troubling Talpade was that the old man did not seem capable enough to add small portions of ricin into each capsule. Whose help would he have taken? Who was his accomplice in the crime?

Even as he was absorbed in these thoughts, his cell phone rang. It was an unknown number. Talpade took the call. A meek voice spoke at the other end. "Hello, sir.

This is Sumitra Desai. I am the accountant who works for *Advent Electronics*. May I meet you, sir? I wanted to tell you something. It may be relevant to your case."

Talpade's heartbeat quickened but he kept calm and said, "Sure, madam. Would you be comfortable coming over to the police station or would you prefer that I came over to your residence? Rest assured, I will come after duty hours tonight, in plain clothes. I will not turn up in my uniform."

After hesitating for a few moments, the lady answered, "Yes, sir. Please do come over tonight. I will message you my address. Not later than 9 though. My children have school and college early in the morning and we turn in to bed by 11 p.m."

"Of course, madam. I understand. I will come there by 9:30 p.m., if that's all right," said the policeman. He tried his best to contain his excitement and curiosity which almost made him wish that he could rush to *Advent Electronics* and interrogate her right away. As he hung up, he reminded himself to be patient. It was already 5:30 p.m. He would need that much time to check the Pranali Dive angle and then reach Sumitra Desai's residence. He got into the jeep and told the driver, "Mahakali Caves Road, Andheri."

6:36 p.m.

Talpade's head was throbbing by the time the jeep pulled into Jeevan Dhara Apartments. He silently cursed Mumbai's traffic as he took the lift. It was a nondescript housing colony and flat number 305 was locked. He rang the neighbour's bell and was told that Mrs. Dive had gone to her native place with her daughter. The neighbour had no idea where that was nor did she know when Mrs. Dive would be back. "This is my number. I need to speak to Mrs. Dive regarding an ongoing investigation. She may have some information so please let me know as soon as she returns," requested Talpade. The middle-aged woman, who had identified herself as Mrs. Gokhale, agreed and the officer got back into his jeep, disappointed that the whole trip had been wasted.

7:16 p.m.

Sumitra trudged along the narrow by lanes of her chawl, fatigued after a hard day's work. Managing a job, her home and the demands of two growing girls was becoming a challenge for her.

As Sumitra entered her modest home, she noticed her elder one, Mohini, playing a game on the mobile phone, oblivious to the world around her. "Beta, get me a glass of water," she said in a tired voice. "Just a second mom," said her daughter, engrossed in her attempt at bettering her earlier record at popping virtual bubbles.

With a sigh, Sumitra got up and filled a tall stainless-steel glass to the brim. Water supply was going to be affected again in the summer months and she would have to get up twice as early in order to fill enough water for the day from the local municipal water pump.

Just as she finished draining her glass of water, Mohini entered and hugged her mother affectionately. "Why do you want every instruction of yours obeyed in the next three seconds, aai? Why can't you wait for a few seconds longer? I can't just drop whatever I am doing and do your bidding straightaway, can I? It makes me feel awful when I see that you have done it yourself!"

Sumitra gave her a wan smile and said, "I guess moms are programmed that way. There is only a three second waiting period after which their brain goes on auto mode! Do it yourself is the best policy, I guess, where mothers are concerned. So, tell me *baccha,* how was your exam today? Did the paper go well? History, *na*?"

Mohini started helping Sumitra clean the spinach leaves for dinner and stood alongside her mom leaning against the kitchen platform. "Yes. It was okay, I guess. The paper was lengthy but predictable. Mom, I wanted to ask you something. Is this a good time?"

"Can it wait till after we finish dinner?" Sumitra replied.

"Sure. No rush. Shall I help you roll the rotis?" Mohini understood that her mother was tired but post dinner, she would be overcome with sleep and then she would not have the heart to sit her down and unburden herself of her trials and tribulations at college. It would have to wait.

Even as she started rolling the rotis, a gruff voice called from the door that was already ajar, "Mrs. Sumitra Desai? May I come in? Inspector Pramod Talpade had arrived 15 minutes earlier than planned.

Sumitra looked at Mohini and said, "Please finish rolling out these rotis. I will add the finishing touches to the dal in a while. I need to talk to this gentleman for a while. It's work-related."

Without really waiting for a response from her daughter, Sumitra signalled to the police officer that he should follow her to the bedroom in order to be out of earshot of her daughter. As she put a lid on the dal, she noticed Mohini's suspicious sidelong glance at the officer. She would have a lot of explaining to do once the officer had left, but it could not be helped. Sighing, she followed the gentleman into the tiny room. The bed was cluttered with exercise books, text books and other paraphernalia. Sumitra swiftly shoved it all into a corner and made space for the man to sit. She parked herself on a makeshift stool that was actually a yellowing thermocol piece. It was an ancient relic from a gift her husband had crafted for their daughters from a block of thermocol. The sight of the stool made her nostalgic about the hop-scotch and snakes and ladders that he played with the two girls using the hand-crafted dice made out of the thermocol block. It was an inexpensive gift but had been a labour of love. The girls refused to part with it and she found it useful as a stool. Brushing aside these thoughts, Sumitra focused on the task at hand.

The officer surveyed the sparse furniture and the littered bed for a moment before he drew out a pen and notepad. "Yes, Mrs. Desai. You had some information to give me. As you know, we are investigating the death of your ex-colleague, Rosy Fernandes. We now believe that it may have been a homicide. Any information that you have for us can help us crack the case so please be honest and don't be afraid."

Sumitra Desai was tired and hungry. Her kids would be ravenous too, so she decided to keep it short and sweet. "It's almost dinner time inspector, and we are all very hungry so I am going to come straight to the point without beating around the bush. I wanted to talk to you about this earlier today when you had come to the office but with everyone else around, I didn't want to attract undue attention."

Talpade nodded and waited patiently. Informants were generally nervous creatures. Unnecessary prodding sometimes led them to clam up. Silence was usually the best resort. Sumitra could feel the dryness in her throat but she resisted the urge to go back into the kitchen to fetch a glass of water. The prospect of fielding curious questions from her elder one was dissuasive enough. Instead, she asked the officer, "Would you like some water sir? Sorry, I forgot my manners. I should have asked you earlier." Strange are the ways of human beings. We project our own desires on to the person sitting in front of us in the hope that they might agree, thus enabling us to achieve what we really want.

The officer politely declined. "No, Mrs. Desai. I am good. Thank you. So, you were saying…?"

Sumitra hesitated and then decided to be brave enough to blurt it all out. "Officer, I joined the company two years ago after my husband's demise. He used to work for *Advent Electronics* as an accountant. I was qualified too but was not really interested in working and we managed with the salary he brought home. Mr. Trivedi had come home to pay his last respects and also to hand over the cheque for the gratuity amount and offered me the job if I so desired. I took him up on the offer as I have two girls who are still in college and school. I needed to work to run the home. I don't know how to say this. I have no proof to give you, no evidence, except my gut feeling, my discomfort, my unease at the whole experience. You must believe me when I tell you this, but Mr. Trivedi is not what he appears to be. Everyone in the office thinks he is the veritable gentleman, well-mannered and polite. But the way he looks at me has always made me uncomfortable. It is only when I am alone in the room with him that I get this feeling. It is an inexplicable feeling of being checked out. I don't know how to explain it to you. When he sits inside his cabin and looks at me through the glass door I feel as if his glance is sizing me up, if you know what I mean. Don't get me wrong. I am not obsessive about these things. I don't feel that way about the other men working in the office. It is just the boss who gives me these vibes."

Talpade realized that she was making a great effort to keep her nerve and that the very act of coming out in the open about these fears was a herculean task for this mother of two struggling to make ends meet. "Did you ever confront him about this, Mrs. Desai?"

"No, officer. I never mustered the courage to do that," replied Sumitra Desai with resignation writ large on her face.

"I see. Did any other female employee of the organization ever share a similar experience with you in these two years? Maybe Rosy Fernandes herself? She was the boss's secretary, wasn't she? She would have worked closely with Mr. Trivedi."

"No. I never really discussed it with anyone. I usually mind my own business and come home directly after work without chit chatting."

"That's all right. I can understand. Tell me, Rosy Fernandes was already working for Mr. Trivedi when you joined the company, correct?"

"Yes. She had over three years of experience back then."

"Was she friendly by nature? Did you ever confide in her perhaps?" asked the officer.

"She was not my type sir. She was fashion conscious and well, not a person who would be interested in interacting with me usually, except where it concerned work. As I worked in the accounts department, I was the one writing out the cheques and managing the bank transactions for the company. So, we interacted only where it was absolutely essential. She managed the appointments, visitors, the boss's personal mail, correspondence and daily schedule."

"Understood. So why did she leave her job?" Talpade asked hopefully. He had actually asked the other employees the same question but they had not really come up with any concrete answers. All he had gleaned was that she had quit the job suddenly. Somehow, he felt he might get some answers from this lady who sensed some kind of sexual harassment at work. It was an inexplicable double-edged sword, this kind of testimony. However, at this stage of the investigation, any information was useful.

Talpade motored on, in spite of his own reservations about the utility of the woman's confession. He resisted the urge to roll his eyes every time she mentioned how her boss looked at her. His mental chatter was immensely distracting. As a man himself, he could not help it. A voice in his head kept saying, "Now we should not even look at you women, is it? Anything the male does is wrong. Of course. What else can one expect from you women?" Shutting the voice in his head, he goaded her on. "Why do you think Ms. Fernandes resigned from her job as secretary to the CEO so suddenly?"

"I have absolutely no idea sir. She did not really talk to me about it. She probably told the boss. He was soft on her. He definitely was. I can give you evidence for this. He made me give her two lakhs in cash. I handed it over to her a fortnight after she had resigned. He also ensured that all her dues were cleared that very month. Now which boss would do so much for a secretary who had quit without even a notice period, tell me? They were definitely making out and she must have been threatening him with consequences. That's why he did all this, so his wife would not find out. I am telling you, she definitely had something up her sleeve." Sumitra Desai said all this with a highly conspiratorial air. Just then, she noticed her daughter out of the corner of her eye and clammed up completely.

"That's all I know, sir. And now, if you will excuse me, I really should get down to making dinner. My kids are hungry." She started twirling the end of her saree pallu. The mother clearly did not want her kid to know all this. He could not just let it go at that. "Mrs. Desai, did you go to Rosy's residence to give her the cash or did she come by the office to collect it?"

"Umm…no. She came to meet the boss on the 2nd of January at 11 a.m. I remember this clearly because the boss' wife had also come to the office for some work that day but then, she got reminded of another appointment and left without meeting her husband. I saw Rosy hand something over to the boss and he gave her the cash. He asked me to keep it ready for her and insisted on handing her the money himself. I had kept the cash ready in a pale green envelope, the kind we use to courier official correspondence and samples."

Talpade's mind raced to the cash found on the victim's person. They had all wondered why Rosy Fernandes had so much cash at her residence and also in her handbag on the day she died at the spa. That was one of the puzzles that he was looking to solve. "Were you able to see what Rosy Fernandes gave your boss that day?" he asked her, trying hard to control his excitement.

"No. It was something really tiny. I could not really make out what it was. That is all I know, sir. I hope I will not get into any trouble for my honesty?" Sumitra Desai asked in a panic-stricken voice.

"Rest assured, madam. No harm will come to you. Thank you for your cooperation. I will get in touch with you again if I need any more information." Talpade politely made his exit after nodding at the girl who stood staring at him.

As he left Sumitra Desai's residence, Talpade reached for his cell. It was time to update Ashutosh about the day's findings. The investigation was heating up but there were many loose ends. His mind was addled and it always helped to talk to his colleague. Talpade respected his assistant. He might not be the fittest of colleagues with his rotund midriff, but his mind was very agile. He was committed and had a great work ethic. It was through conversations with Ashutosh in the past that he had thought of new leads. Years of experience had taught Ashutosh Dubey not to get excited by theories unless they were accompanied by hard evidence. Nothing short of concrete data and proof held water in a court of law.

9:39 p.m.

Ashutosh Dubey was in the midst of planning his vacation with the family when Talpade's call came through. His wife, Sneha, groaned when he took the call. With a sheepish yet apologetic grin, the man disappeared behind the curtain into his tiny balcony and said, "Yes, as per your instructions, I sent the whitish powder across to Dr. Phadnavis through Havaldar Shetty for testing in the afternoon itself. He gave me a verbal report over the telephone at around 7:15 this evening, confirming that it was ricin. The actual typed report will be handed over tomorrow morning. What happened at *Advent Electronics*?"

"A lot, Ashutosh, a lot. While we were leaving the office, Mr. Trivedi's accountant, a lady named Sumitra Desai, expressed a desire to share some information. She seemed nervous and so I handed over a chit with my number on it. She called me up later in the day, gave me her address and suggested that I visit her after 7 p.m. So, I went to see her as planned. I have taken her testimony down and wanted to run a few things past you. I am sorry to have disturbed you at home but there are some things that don't seem to be tying up. Can you come over to the station so we can discuss this in person? We keep getting interrupted with other things, so I thought perhaps we could meet after dinner today."

Talpade was disappointed with Ashutosh's reply. "Not now Pramod. The family is having a discussion. We are planning the annual vacation for the summer and I will have no peace if I interrupt it to discuss another case. You will not understand my situation till you get married yourself, Pramod."

Saying this, the weary officer hung up only to find his wife within earshot, facing him with her arms akimbo, glaring accusingly at him. Grinning at her, he apologized to the children who had gone back to the books they were reading on their phones, habituated to these interruptions. His wife, however, was another story. Eager to make amends, he quickly took up from where he had left off, "Sorry about that interruption. Yes, so as I was saying, we have two options, we either take a fast train to Jaipur that does not halt anywhere else or take the second option that is much slower. What do you feel?"

Friday, 30th April

9:48 p.m.

The case had progressed rapidly. Inspector Talpade was disgusted by the old man. Hemant Trivedi was guilty of violating the Information Act Section 66E and he would now be tried by a court of law. No one, not even his lawyer could save him now. Unless a well-wisher bailed him out of prison, the man was doomed. The number of well-wishers that Hemant Trivedi was left with would dwindle further, he surmised, when the facts of the case were made public.

The man's wife would be appalled at the news of her husband's lewd behaviour. The man probably had no friends. Shrikant Atre was an exception, but after Talpade's recent interrogation, the Inspector was doubtful that the man would want anything to do with Hemant Trivedi. He might have unsuspecting relatives who might bail him out though. Putting these thoughts away, the officer brought his complete attention to the situation at hand.

The evidence was indeed damning but somehow Inspector Talpade had not been convinced. "Ashutosh, how can a 65-year-old man have the steadiness to carry out such a meticulous task? Separating capsules, replacing the ricin with the asthalin and then replacing the capsules the way they were while wearing gloves requires a steady hand."

Ashutosh Dubey wholeheartedly agreed, "You are absolutely right, but who else could have done it? Do you think he had someone to help him in the task? I don't think he would have roped anyone else in. It would mean confessing his crime to another person. That is a risk he would surely not take."

Pramod Talpade sighed tiredly. "Let's call it a day Ashutosh. See you tomorrow."

Saturday, 19th June

7:30 a.m.

The man he was chasing was getting away from him. Talpade ran furiously to catch him. He was short of breath and sweat obstructed his view. He followed his quarry relentlessly. Suddenly, the man stopped in his tracks, swerved and faced Talpade. He was brandishing a knife. Before Talpade could gather his wits, the man stabbed him viciously several times. Pain shot through him. He yelled and tried to stop the man but he had run away. Sweating profusely, Talpade tried to reach for his mobile. Even as he made a painful effort, he could hear his mobile ring.

As he reached for his cell phone, he realized that this was just a dream. His mobile was ringing and had just awakened him from a terrible nightmare. He looked at the time. He was late. Groggily, he answered the call from an unknown number.

“Good morning, sir. This is Mrs. Gokhale.”

“Mrs. Gokhale? I am afraid I don’t recognize you.”

“I am Mrs. Gokhale from Jeevan Dhara Apartments. Pranali Dive’s neighbour. You had given me your number and had asked me to inform you when she returns. Remember me? Well, Mrs. Dive has returned at around 6:30 this morning.”

"Ah, yes. I recollect now. Yes, Mrs. Gokhale. Thank you so much for the information. I will be there in a while." Talpade was wide awake. The lady had finally returned.

Talpade was wide awake now and eager to follow up on this lead. The Rosy Fernandes case had been closed with the arrest of Hemant Trivedi. But as far as Inspector Patwardhan and Talpade were concerned, the case was far from closed. They were sure that there was a missing link that they had to uncover. Was Pranali Dive going to shed some light on this missing link? The restlessness that accompanied all unsolved mysteries had been intruding into his sleep for the past few months and he wanted to close this file once and for all.

On reaching the police station, he briefed his boss and set off for Andheri along with a lady constable in the police jeep. It was almost 10:30 a.m. when he reached Jeevan Dhara apartments. Seeing him in uniform, the watchman immediately escorted him to the flat.

The lady who greeted him was in her late thirties. "Madam, good morning. I am inspector Pramod Talpade from the Bandra West Police Station. I am here in connection with an investigation. I have some questions pertaining to Mr. Hemant Trivedi. May I come in?" asked Talpade.

Mrs. Dive's face turned ashen at the mention of Hemant Trivedi. Soundlessly, she let him and the constable inside and shut the door when she saw her neighbour peep into the flat.

“Yes, officer. What is it that you want to know?” The lady’s manner seemed to have suddenly changed. She had become strangely quiet and moody.

Talpade did not beat around the bush. “How are you related to Mr. Trivedi, Mrs. Dive?”

Instead of answering Talpade, she turned on him with a counter question, “Who has directed you to me? How did you find me?”

“That is not of any concern to you, madam. The police have their own methods. If you withhold any information, we will arrest you and take you to the police station for further questioning, madam. An enquiry is in progress and anyone obstructing the smooth conduct of the enquiry is liable to be arrested for questioning. Please cooperate.” Talpade was firm but gentle.

The lady was clearly worried. Tears started streaming down her cheeks. Talpade gave her some water to drink from a jug kept nearby and waited patiently for her to calm down.

The lady constable sat next to Mrs. Dive and put an arm around her shoulder. “Please answer the questions honestly and we will leave quietly. There is no need to panic. If you are innocent, no harm will come to you. It is sensible to cooperate.”

After sipping on the water, Pranali Dive began her tale. “I met Mr. Trivedi for the first time at a crossing. I almost fainted in the middle of the road and he was at the wheel of his car. Fortunately for me, he applied the brakes on time and got me admitted to a hospital. He took care of me till I recovered. At that time, I did not know that he was married. We met six years ago. We started dating and he kept me completely in the dark about his marital status. In him I found a lover as well as a father figure I had never had the good fortune to experience. It was only when I was pregnant with my child that he told me he was married. He wanted me to have this child. He was childless and wanted to father the child. But he was not willing to marry me. I would have a flat in my name, he promised and assured me that he would look after the baby and provide for our upkeep. I had no option but to agree. He was very loving towards me and I agreed reluctantly. We would have fights now and then but he always managed to pacify me. We took great care to keep our affair quiet. How did you come to know of it? Did he tell you?"

"No madam. Are you aware that Mr. Trivedi has been arrested?" asked Talpade, looking at her questioningly. He was amazed that anyone could be so naive in the twenty first century and blindly trust a man who was clearly two-timing her.

The lady was shocked to hear this. "What?"

"How frequently did he visit you?" asked Talpade, undeterred by her shocked expression.

"He hasn't been coming here for the last eight to nine months. He used to send a gentleman named Shrikant Atre who works in his company to my place with cash."

"Has it never occurred to you that he was sending you money in cash through this man to avoid a paper trail?

Mr. Atre is of the opinion that Mr. Trivedi was helping a poor woman. Are you happy with this life, Mrs. Dive? Did you never confront Mrs. Trivedi or apprise her of your existence?"

"I threatened to do that several times, officer, but he would always manage to pacify me with his love and gifts. I have had a very difficult childhood and this was a love I did not want to lose. He was also a very loving father to my child and doted on us. He always told us that he was preoccupied with his business and that was the reason for his prolonged absences. Whenever I would ask him about his wife, he would say that she had no time for him, that she was immersed in academics and had lost interest in sex."

Pranali Dive wrung her hands anxiously as she asked the inspector, "What has he been arrested for? What has he done? What will become of us now?" She broke down completely.

"He has been arrested on charges of filming three teenagers in stages of undress, obviously violating their privacy. Do you want to meet him? Would you be interested in applying for bail so that he can join you here?" Talpade baited her.

"I cannot believe this, but if it is true I want nothing to do with the man. I will never trust my child with him. No, I don't want to see him, let alone get him out on bail. I just hope and pray that he will leave us in peace and never trouble us."

The police officer was incredulous. How could this woman allow herself to be cheated in this fashion? Was she truly gullible or was she trying to put on an act? He decided that planting a tail on her residence would be necessary and as they walked down the staircase, he told the lady constable to hang around and report to him in the evening as to Mrs. Dive's movements.

As the jeep hurtled towards the city, Talpade's expression was grim. Hemant Trivedi was no good Samaritan. He was a lecherous old man who had deceived this poor woman. He could not help but wonder how Shrikant Atre had been fooled by the old man. Did he not have the brains to put two and two together? Hemant Trivedi had been harbouring a mistress all along without his wife's knowledge. If the Rosy Fernandes case had not come out into the open, this affair would never have come to light either. It was a sad business, this case. If they did not succeed in finding incriminating evidence against the man, he would probably be let off with just a five-year jail term. They had to nail him for the murder of Rosy Fernandes to ensure that he served a life sentence. To top it all, the police would have to perform the unpleasant task of informing Mrs. Trivedi that her husband had a mistress with an illegitimate daughter, stowed away in Andheri. The loyalties of the mistress and her daughter would, at best, be considered suspicious. Otherwise, he was friendless. At least, investigations so far had not thrown up any bosom pals.

Sunday, 27th June

9:30 a.m.

It was pouring as if there was going to be no abatement. Laasya had taken refuge in the spa because she had been caught unawares by the downpour. She had an interview at the Bandra Kurla Complex and on the way impulsively decided to stop over for a facial. Anyway, she did not want to get drenched before an interview. The facial would give her some time and she wanted to feel confident. It was a Multinational Pharma firm that was looking for a biotechnologist and Laasya fit the bill perfectly. The interview was at 12:30. There was ample time and she was early. The staff at the salon hadn't even reported for work yet. What was she going to do to kill time? Impatiently, she fiddled with her phone, checking her WhatsApp chats and decided to talk to Pramod. It was a while since they had exchanged notes. This was an officer of the law she genuinely liked. He had no airs about himself and was a down to earth guy who did not fawn over her as most of her other acquaintances did.

He did not answer his phone, so Laasya surveyed the place for lack of better things to do. Slowly she realized that this was the very same parlour where the Rosy Fernandes murder had taken place. Pramod had discussed the case with her about three months ago. Due to insufficient evidence, the accused had been acquitted and it was only because there was no one to bail him out of Section 66E that he had been put behind bars for six months. Pramod had been very disappointed that they had not managed to conclusively prove that the accused, Hemant Trivedi, Proprietor of *Advent Electronics*, had committed a premeditated crime by murdering Rosy Fernandes. They had not been able to come up with any concrete evidence and the defence had proved beyond doubt that a man whose hand was not even steady enough to hold a pencil and sign steadily, could hardly have filled asthalin capsules with the poison ricin, replaced the caps and thus successfully poisoned his blackmailer to get her out of his way.

This was a loophole that had been gnawing at Pramod for over three months and the case had not yet been resolved. If she remembered right, it was *Clara's Spa* in Bandra and that was exactly where she was, coincidentally. As she looked around, she saw a short, petite woman arranging bronze cups on the wall in a reductionist pattern. She was busy pasting star anise in a circular pattern in one of the cups. Meticulously, she pasted each one using an adhesive and then proceeded to do the same with cardamom pods, cloves, bay leaves and then star anise once again in an alternative pattern. When she turned around, Laasya noticed the name *Renu* embroidered on the pocket to the right-hand side of her uniform.

Just then her phone rang. Pramod Talpade. She smiled as she took the call. "Hi boss! *Kidhar hai tu*? It's been ages. Guess where I am currently? You have three guesses."

"*Arre pooch mat*. I have been extremely busy. Neck deep in work. The crime scene is getting worse every year. This year has been particularly brutal. Murders galore. The unsolved crimes file is growing thicker," replied inspector Talpade, internally very glad that Laasya had remembered him. This was a welcome break from his routine. "I am never good at guessing games. Please tell me. Where are you?"

Gleefully, Laasya declared, "I am at *Clara's Spa*. Yes, the same spa which was the site of that murder you were working on some time ago. That ricin poisoning case you were discussing with me the last time we met. Rosy Fernandes, I think, the victim's name was. Tell me, did you solve that case at all or is it also one of those unsolved cases lying there piled up on your desk?"

"Please don't joke about this, Laasya. It's not funny. We were this close to cracking that case. However, the prosecution could not justify its stand and we had no evidence to show that someone had helped Hemant Trivedi to commit the crime. Sadly, he will go scot free in a few more months. It enrages me so much!"

"Sorry Pramod. I didn't mean to be insensitive. Do let me know if I can help in some way with any of our other cases or even this one. Such lecherous humans should never be released. Would you like me to investigate anything for you here while I am waiting for my facial? The staff here hasn't arrived yet. There is just one girl, named Renu, who is dusting the place currently."

"Oh! Renu was a key witness in the case. No, there is nothing you or anyone can do about that case Laasya, I am afraid, nothing can be done."

Pramod hung up after making some polite enquiries about Laasya's folks and job prospects. Poor Pramod, he sounded very low. If only she could help him and the police with their investigation. As Laasya put her cell phone back inside her handbag, she felt a hand on her shoulder.

Startled, she looked up only to see Renu signal something to her. She followed her inside the cabin. Having reached the cabin, Renu spoke to Laasya in a hushed voice. "Madam, I could not help but overhear what you were telling your inspector friend. That gentleman was a nice man. He tried to find the reason behind the death of Rosy Fernandes. My co-worker Akshara told me before leaving the job that Clara Madam tampered with some crucial evidence. I don't exactly think she was wrong but I want to tell you the truth because I am going to leave this job soon. I am only working through my notice period. I have nothing to lose now. Actually, when Rosy Fernandes was found dead, just before the police arrived, our boss, Clara D'Souza, threw out the residual water in the steamer because there were some dust particles floating in it. It is possible that someone had poisoned that water as well with something else and the capsules that she inhaled only worsened the situation. However, I have no proof of the matter. This is just something that has been troubling me ever since that ill-fated day in April. Another weird little fact that I did not share with the police during their investigation is that the last client who had a facial in this cabin at around 5 p.m. the previous evening, insisted on having the cup that held the water inside the steamer cleaned thoroughly, dried and replaced before her facial because she was apparently allergic to dust and had sensitive skin. I thought it was strange then but did not bring it up as I did not want the Salon to come under any kind of radar. Please don't put me in any trouble because of what I have said. I just want the culprits brought to book. That's all. I don't want to get embroiled in any controversy or police enquiry."

Laasya quickly reassured her that she would not get into any trouble for her honesty, took her personal mobile number and address and after being reassured that she would testify to this in a court of law, let Renu go back to her chores. By then the other members of the staff started reporting to work. Laasya changed into a gown and thoughtfully lay down for a relaxing facial, eager to share this discovery with Pramod.

The facial took longer than expected but the results were stunning. Laasya was more than happy with the way she looked. She was feeling self-indulgent and so she opted for a quick hair wash and blow dry. She was now ready to take on the world. Confident of acing the interview, she instructed the rickshaw driver, "BKC lena, bhaiyya! Zara jaldi." As the rickshaw hurtled onwards, Laasya reached for her mobile. As usual, he did not take her call. He must be in the midst of another one of his unsolved cases, it was best to send him a text. It had to be dramatic enough to ensure he did not make any excuses and reschedule. She drafted her message with care.

Am going to BKC for an interview. Meet me at Surmai for lunch at 3. I have some breaking news for you. It may help you solve one of your unsolved cases! Be there on time. Kanjoos! I know what you are thinking. Don't worry. We're going to split the bill.

She sent an SMS as she was aware that police work often took Pramod into territory with either very poor or no network at all. That done, she mentally prepared herself for a gruelling time.

The interview went well. The panellists were impressed with her smart replies and appearance. Her overall personality and her thorough knowledge of the subject impressed them just as much as the confidence she exuded. She negotiated hard and reached the restaurant as planned fifteen minutes earlier than expected.

She carefully selected a table at the far end of the restaurant, secluded enough to seat two individuals who wanted to chat in peace without being disturbed. Laasya had chosen this restaurant because their seafood was delectable and their service slow. After reserving the table, she waited impatiently for Pramod to arrive.

3:43 p.m.

When Talpade finally arrived, Laasya took one look at his tired and harried condition and decided against reproaching him for his late arrival. "Hi! What's up? I have taken the liberty to order some soup and starters so we can start talking over food. You can choose the main course," she said, deliberately, keeping her tone light and carefree. His expression betrayed his emotional state more explicitly than ever before.

"Thanks for taking the initiative to order the soup and starters, *yaar*! I am starving. I haven't eaten since eight in the morning. So, tell me, what was the surprising update you wanted to give me?" said Talpade, tucking into the paneer chilly and fish fingers with gusto.

"Well, Renu approached me after I finished talking to you and she spilled some beans. I don't know what came over her or whether she had any ulterior motive for doing so, but let me first tell you what she said. Apparently, Clara D'Souza emptied the water inside the steamer for fear that the police will question her for using contaminated water during steaming. It seems there were some dust particles floating in the water and she did not want the Spa's reputation to be compromised. So basically, your evidence was tampered with. This means that the possibility that the water in the steamer had been poisoned as well cannot be ruled out entirely."

Talpade almost choked on the fish fingers! "What a silly woman! Couldn't she have told us this during our interrogation? We would have explored this angle as well with the forensics. Damn that Renu!"

"Go easy on those curses, Pramod. Any person in their right mind will try to protect herself. She has proved to be useful, though late, in her confession. She has helped shed new light on the case." said Laasya. "She told me that the day prior to Rosy Fernandes' death, the client who had come in for a facial at around 4 p.m. had insisted repeatedly that the steamer and the cup containing the water be cleaned thoroughly before the facial was administered to her. Some Mrs. Khan, apparently, a regular customer, almost as regular as Rosy herself, it seems. That was why the water container inside the steamer was not cleaned out as Akshara had just done it the day before. Renu mentioned this as a very strange incident because never before had anyone insisted on such a thing. I also found this very weird and so I went ahead to do some investigating on my own. When the receptionist was busy attending to another client, I took some pictures of the entries on their appointment diary for the period between October and March. I discovered a curious pattern. Every time Rosy Fernandes visited the parlour, Mrs. Khan was there too. This has happened at least eight times between October and April. It is too frequent and systematic to be a coincidence; don't you think?" said Laasya as she gave her phone to Pramod.

Talpade's face was grim as he scrolled through the entries. "You are absolutely right, Laasya! This is brilliant work! Super deduction! You should join our team actually. Why don't you speak to Dr. Milind? I am sure he will be more than happy to recruit you. He needs an assistant very badly at the moment."

"Focus on the case, Pramod. See, the pattern emerges very clearly. Mrs. Khan seems to figure only on those times when Rosy herself has an appointment. It's very systematic. There seems to be a clear method to Mrs. Khan's modus operandi. You will have to check with the staff there whether the lady wore a burkha. Even if she did, the person doing the facial would have got a good look at her face. You have your perpetrator here. Perhaps Rosy Fernandes was a habitual blackmailer. The senior Trivedi was not the only person who wanted her dead. This Mrs. Khan has her own motive and that's what you need to figure out!" said Laasya smugly as she dug into the prawn peas pulav and *surmai* with relish. She was determined to have her own start up as a Private Eye and was in no mood to play second fiddle to anyone else when she could be her own boss.

Talpade looked at Laasya admiringly and agreed with the sprightly girl's theory, "Hmm… you have a point there. I think it would be best to get Renu to describe Mrs. Khan to our sketch artist. That way, we will get something to work on. I will head for the Spa after our lunch is done. It will be a punishment to do legwork of any kind after this meal. I have overeaten! Thanks for reviving this case! We badly needed a breakthrough on at least one case to keep up our flagging spirits. The Department is facing a lot of flak."

As Laasya turned over the menu to check out the dessert, Talpade found himself trying very hard not to stare at her beautiful *jhumkas* that swayed with every motion and the stray strands of her hair that she kept tucking behind her ears.

5:45 p.m.

Talpade hovered outside the spa as he waited for an opportunity to interview Renu without anyone noticing. An hour had elapsed. His patience was rewarded when

Renu herself emerged. She disappeared into the restaurant a few metres away. As she finished placing an order for snacks and some tea for herself and her colleagues, she found that she did not have change.

Talpade offered her change and politely said, "Good evening, Renu ji. I hope you recognize me? If you don't mind, I have a request to make. I won't take much time. After work today, please come to the police station. Our sketch artist will be there and all you need to do is describe Mrs. Khan to him. We are exploring this angle. Thank you for all your help. Please cooperate with us so that justice is done and we catch the killer."

Seeing the look of alarm on her face, Talpade reassured her with, "Don't worry. There will be no trouble for you or your Spa. We are only trying to ascertain the identity of Mrs. Khan. The telephone number given seems to be a fake one. We suspect that she is somehow involved with the murder of Rosy Fernandes. It is a cold-blooded murder and your description will help us solve the case. Please assist us."

Renu sighed and resigned herself to her fate. She did not protest when the inspector offered to pay for the snacks and tea. She should have known that the casual conversation with Dr. Laasya earlier that morning was going to lead to consequences. She didn't expect Mumbai Police to be so quick however and was unpleasantly surprised. She decided that after helping the police figure out how Mrs. Khan looked it would be best to leave this job and lie low for a while. She would have to look for another job in a hurry. Clara D'Souza would never give her a good reference if she found out that

Renu had squealed to the police about the water in the steamer being emptied out after Rosy Fernandes died.

9:00 p.m.

Laasya had just gone into the shower, tired, after a rather hectic day when she heard her cell buzz. She hit pause on the EDM that she was listening to and took the call. It was Pramod. "*Bol*! What's up?"

The excitement in Talpade's voice was palpable. "You are never going to believe this! The sketch artist has finished his portrait after listening to Renu's description of Mrs. Khan. It is Mrs. Prerna Trivedi, Hemant Trivedi's wife. This is a revelation! I am so tempted to go and interrogate her with all this information right away but it would not be appropriate. It will only give her a chance to escape tonight. Tomorrow is also a Sunday. What say, we meet for breakfast tomorrow and visit her just like that?"

"I don't think that will be such a good idea, Pramod. She will still get a chance to escape if she is alerted on a Sunday, assuming she has a role to play in all this. It would be better to do a background check on her first. Let's meet after you have done a background check on her thoroughly. Collect as much information as possible about her. Professors have a lot of information displayed on their institution's website. Take a look and then let us plan a strategy carefully. Otherwise, as you just said, she will disappear."

Talpade signed off after wishing Laasya goodnight and then started scouring the college website for information on Professor Prerna Trivedi. As he looked her up, he saw several research papers published by her listed under her achievements:

"A Study of Bioactive Compounds from Plant Associated Fungi from the Western Ghats."

"Epigenetic Approaches for Metabolite Diversification to enhance the diversity of Bioactive Compounds."

"A Study of the Utility of Biomarkers as Quality Control Indices for Polyherbal Formulations."

"Metabolomic Profiling and the future of Nutraceuticals."

"The Interaction Between Metabolites and Proteins: A Chromatographic Analysis."

"The Efficacy of Natural Products and the Role Played by Clustered Regularly Interspaced Short Palindromic Repeats."

"The Global Natural Food Colour Market and the Market Research Report of 2016: An Analysis."

Her areas of interest seemed to be varied, including Biotechnology, Biochemistry, Nutraceutics and Chemistry. She would definitely be well versed with toxins. Ricin was a common enough toxin.

Monday, 28th June

Talpade had spent a restless night. He hurriedly ate a couple of chappatis left over from dinner for breakfast with some pickle and rushed to the housing complex where the Trivedis lived. He was hoping to interrogate the girls who were their paying guests after speaking to Prerna Trivedi. Even after multiple rings, no one answered the door. Frustrated, he rang the neighbour's bell. He flashed his ID as he was in mufti and explained the situation to the middle-aged man who had opened the door. The man reluctantly called the policeman inside. Talpade got straight to the point.

"This is the police. No one seems to be answering the doorbell of your neighbour's house. Have they gone out somewhere?"

The man looked surprised and said, "Oh, so you don't know? Mrs. Trivedi died soon after her husband was arrested. She had been hospitalized due to Covid. Respiratory failure, it seems."

The news took Talpade by surprise. Prerna Trivedi? Dead? This was unbelievable. She had seemed absolutely hale and hearty when he interrogated her just a few months back. He controlled himself and went on to ask a few more questions of the neighbour.

"What about those three girls who lived with them as paying guests? Where have they gone?"

"No idea, sir. The girls didn't tell us anything. They just handed the keys of the flat to us and left. They must have gone to their respective homes, I guess."

Talpade decided to go back to the police station, get the girls' contact numbers and trace their whereabouts.

It was almost 9:30 when he finally met them at a restaurant. He had spent the day tracing them. Inspector Pramod Talpade was exhausted. He had called Laasya to the restaurant, for company and because he thought her presence would calm the girls down. Talking to a policeman can make any one anxious.

The girls were frank in stating the facts of the case. Talpade and Laasya listened intently.

Rehana could not help crying as she recollected the events that had unfolded on that fateful day when Prerna Trivedi had first taken ill.

She recounted how she along with Binaz, and Vinita had arranged for an ambulance to admit their teacher to Gemini Hospital, the one closest to their house. The retired professor had lost her sense of taste and smell and her fever was showing no sign of abating. She did not want to take any risks due to the pandemic and had isolated herself. The ambulance had arrived in an hour or so. Luckily for them, Gemini was a Covid Hospital.

Vinita gave her a bottle of water to drink as Rehana continued to narrate the sad tale, "At the hospital, the emergency staff was efficient. They wheeled ma'am into the casualty and from there to the ICU. The doctor on duty was quick in his diagnosis. Pulmonary distress. We took turns outside the ICU, entering only to hand over medicines. Sir, it was very distressing to see the woman who had been a mother figure to us for the past year lie helpless and vulnerable on the bed, strung up with all kinds of tubes and machines."

"I understand," said Talpade. "How many days was she in hospital?"

"Well, sir, she was in the ICU for a fortnight or so and then succumbed to respiratory failure. At least that was what the doctors told us. She would call us sometimes from the ICU. During one of her calls, she mentioned a friend, named Akhila, whom she wanted us to inform about her hospitalization and her having contracted Covid. Apparently, she had tried repeatedly but could not get through. She messaged us her number," said Rehana.

Talpade immediately drew out his cell phone and noted the name down as he enquired, "And did you inform Akhila, her friend? What was her reaction?"

"No, sir," the girl continued, "We could not really get through to her. Her phone was switched off most times. But we kept trying and finally we managed to inform her but it was some days later. She was devastated. Said something about being raised in an orphanage with madam in her childhood."

"Do share this lady's number Ms. Rehana. I will have to interrogate her and find out all I can. Thank you for updating us." Inspector Talpade held his cap in his hands, twirling it restlessly as he said, "In case you remember anything else, do let us know. You have been very helpful."

Laasya looked at Talpade inquisitively and the two friends rode home silently lost in their respective thoughts. Talpade dropped Laasya at her residence and went home perturbed by the turn of events. He had almost cracked the case and now his suspected murderer was dead. What was this? Divine justice? Or just a curious turn of events?

As soon as Talpade reached home, he received a text from Rehana. He instantly dialed the number Rehana has just sent him. The call was answered immediately by a confident sounding woman. Akhila worked for *Thanal* an NGO. She was working in Bangalore and would be travelling to Mumbai for some work next week. She said she would not mind coming down to the police station for an interaction.

Akhila kept her word. The very next week she landed at the police station and told the inspector that she would prefer to talk over lunch at a restaurant. Inspector Pramod decided to call Laasya along and the three of them went to a Chinese restaurant around the corner.

As they placed their order for food, Talpade requested Akhila, "Please allow me to record this because we will need your testimony."

Akhila's eyes narrowed. "No inspector. I would not like this conversation recorded. Please listen to what I have to say first. I think I have every right to respect my friend's last wishes."

What she narrated was a sordid tale. Inspector Talpade went straight home and penned down the day's events on his diary. This was a case that had been niggling away at his conscience and Akhila's testimony had finally clarified the puzzle.

Akhila's Testimony:

On 25th April 2021, at around 10:25 pm, just after I had retired for the night, I received a call from Prerna, my best friend, whom I have known from my childhood. She sounded agitated. She said to me, "Akhila, I have a confession to make. My husband. He's innocent. It was me. I killed Rosy Fernandes and framed him for it."

Monday, 5th July

Akhila paused, drank some water and continued, "Inspector, please hear me out completely, before you judge my friend. She has not had a happy marriage and has never been able to give 100 percent of herself to the relationship. Physical intimacy has always been something difficult, even impossible to reconcile with. At least Prerna tried. I never even considered the possibility of a marriage for myself. Visions of Mr. Patel fondling her as a child in the night, the smell of paan that each one of us in the orphanage had to learn to deal with as they were forced to kiss him goodbye were all firmly entrenched in her mind as indeed, they were, in mine as well. Apparently, these unpleasant memories would muscle their way into her mental space every time Hemant tried to get intimate with her and somehow over the years, the husband realized that his wife was not at all comfortable in bed. He had tried to rationalize this with her. She had never been open about this. Never wanted to get her fears and ghosts out in the open. He was therefore unaware of her private battles. He was cold towards Prerna. Ten years after their marriage, they were childless and disconnected. Polite conversation and civility in public was a façade she was finding quite challenging to maintain. Hemant was not even trying to be civil anymore. He was downright rude and often aggressive with her. She felt guilty for not trying enough and blamed herself for making their relationship toxic, for not being able to talk about it.

She accidentally overheard a conversation between Rosy Fernandes and Hemant when she had gone to visit her husband in his office. He was oblivious of her presence and she was in the toilet the whole time overhearing the conversation. Initially, she assumed that Rosy was blackmailing her boss and thought Hemant had had an affair with his secretary. After listening some more, she realized that Rosy had stumbled upon a pen drive that contained some footage of women undressing in front of the mirror. She was shocked out of her wits when she realized that she was living with a sick man. She blamed herself for his behavior somewhere. Socially conditioned into the belief that it was a wife's duty to satisfy every one of her husband's desires. She was confused. She did not know what to do. She did not want to go to the police. She had no proof but decided to take matters into her own hands. Rosy was to her, just as culpable. She should have ideally gone to the police. The despicable secretary was actually making most of a situation where her boss found his reputation compromised. In order to maintain public face, he would give her what she asked and therefore Rosy was blackmailing him. A plan started forming in Prerna's head, one that would punish Rosy by murdering her, one that would punish Hemant for abusing innocent women. One that would send Hemant behind bars for a murder he did not commit. A plan she would execute to perfection. No clues that would lead to her. Every clue would lead the police to Hemant and even if he denied it, he could never prove otherwise.

She had been following Rosy. She studied her routine. Her habits. She decided to become a member of the same beauty parlour Rosy frequented. After six months of scouting, she actioned her plan. She bought a bottle of asthalin capsules, replaced the asthalin in the capsules meticulously with ricin which she had sourced from one of her doctoral students' lab stores. She worked with gloves apparently and ensured that she planted the remainder of the stuff in Hemant Trivedi's office during one of her visits. She had taken an appointment for 5 pm the day before Rosy Fernandes died and had mixed some of the ricin in the steamer after ensuring that it was cleaned by the staff in the parlour. As the ricin was in a powdered form it must have dissolved completely by the next day. She had planned it all knowing full well that the next person to occupy the cabin would be Rosy first thing in the morning. The appointment had been carefully engineered by Prerna so that she would be the last person to leave the spa on the penultimate day. Prerna knew that Covid Protocol would ensure that the beautician administering the facial would wear a mask herself and thus no other casualty would materialize. Prerna knew about Rosy Fernandes' medical history because of some staff get together where she had witnessed an asthmatic attack triggered by dhoop sticks. She called her husband's office staff to their home for a party to celebrate her promotion as Head of the Department. Rosy Fernandes came too. After the party when she visited the restroom, without her knowledge, Prerna substituted the medicine in her handbag that she used for inhaling with a bottle that contained ricin. As planned, Rosy Fernandes succumbed to the ricin. What my dear friend had not bargained for was the guilt that would wrack her mentally. However, the day you visited her home for investigation and took away what looked like a charger, she realized to her horror that her husband was actually secretly filming these unsuspecting girls. She was horrified. She realized then that both her husband and Rosy deserved their fate.

Now I have told you everything. Prerna, my friend, my dear, brave friend, is at peace now. You have no proof and I do not wish to testify. Let sleeping dogs lie sir."

Talpade bid Akhila goodbye with a warm handshake. As the autorickshaw swung its way out of the building, Talpade could not help thinking that Prerna Trivedi was finally resting in one of the most restful but unusual beauty sleeps ever.

www.ingramcontent.com/pod-product-compliance
Ingram Content Group UK Ltd.
Pitfield, Milton Keynes, MK11 3LW, UK
UKHW021935190726
13853UKWH00004B/1468

9 789392 878565